EMBRACE THE LIE(S)

In Golf Or Life, A Lie Is A Lie!

"'Embrace The Lie(s)' isn't just a story—it's the queue line that snakes through Noah Philter's twisted world of golf and politics, priming you for the main event. In this prelude, where every lie is a hazard, we set the stage for the wild ride that awaits in our next thrilling installment ~

'Embrace The Viruses'"

*This is a day in the life of
Noah Philter and the
Encyclopedia for the Political Lust Series.*

Seer K. Facet

About the Author

Seer K. Facet is a self-proclaimed keen observer of life. Born and raised in a tranquil community along the Great Lakes, Facet's early life was shaped by a deep appreciation for nature and community. After exploring various careers, Facet found his calling in promoting tourism and advocating for environmentally responsible practices. However, as he studied the human experience and reflected on the various injustices that have shaped our world, he became increasingly driven to speak out against the systemic failures and moral ambiguities that threaten our collective future. Through his writing, Facet hopes to inspire a new generation of activists, thinkers, and changemakers to join the fight for a more just, equitable, and sustainable world. His debut novel, EMBRACE THE LIES, is a scathing satire that lays bare the dark underbelly of American politics and the perils of unchecked personal freedom.

About Characteristic 26

Characteristic 26™ is a new publishing brand that presents the alphabet 'Shaken, Stirred, And Fused ᔆᔆᴹ'. We're committed to bringing you a curious mix of works that challenge, inspire, provoke, spark conversations, and ignite imaginations as long as we, the people, don't need a king's permit to read them. Our first imprint, Faction Niche, will proudly introduce a new generation of authors and co-authors who boldly tackle tough topics, push the boundaries of satire and social commentary, and/or craft entertaining stories that delight and captivate readers. With EMBRACE THE LIES and its forthcoming sequel, EMBRACE THE VIRUSES, Faction Niche is leading the charge in a new era of innovative and thought-provoking literature. Join us on this exciting journey and discover the unique voices and perspectives that Characteristic 26 has to offer.

Acknowledgments

To the authors of the absurd, the peddlers of propaganda, and the masters of misinformation: thank you for the inspiration. May your fact-free fantasies continue to fuel our satire. To the friends and family who endured my rants, raves, and early-morning writing sessions, your tolerance is appreciated, and how you stayed sane despite my onslaught of chatter is commendable.

Special thanks to my incredible team of assistants, Eirene, Oscar, Etnt, Kate, and my noetic team, who helped bring this absurdity to life. Your dedication and hard work are truly valued.

And to the tens of thousands of people I've had the privilege of conversing with over the years — from all walks of life, with diverse perspectives and opinions — I thank you for sharing your stories, your hopes, and your fears. Your collective desire for a life free from strife and filled with understanding is the true inspiration behind this book. Most of all, I acknowledge the profound truth that the human experience is a human construct built by humans and sometimes wrecked by humans. I believe that we, as a human race, have the capacity to do better, to learn from our mistakes, and to evolve faster. May this book inspire us to question, seek, and create a world that is more just, more compassionate, and more authentic. Lastly, to the generations of young people who refuse to be swayed by the noise and chaos, who seek truth and authenticity, and who strive to make a positive impact on the world — this book is for you. May it inspire you to keep questioning, seeking, and embracing the complexity of our world. Voting is your superpower! To my beta readers of

'Embrace The Viruses' who said that the book needed an introduction, which is 'Embrace The Lies!'

***

This book is a work of fiction. Names, characters, places, and incidents are either products of the author's imagination or, if real, are used fictitiously. Any resemblance to actual persons, living or dead, events, or locales is entirely coincidental. While the narrative may at times seem to parallel real-world events, it is important to remember that this is a satirical work. The author does not intend to make accusations against any real individuals or organizations, nor should the book be taken as a factual account of any events, past or present.

The scenarios presented, including but not limited to the unconventional golf tournament and the fictional political parties, are purely imaginative constructs designed for entertainment purposes. They are not meant to be interpreted as commentary on or predictions of real-world occurrences. Readers are encouraged to approach this book with a sense of humor and an understanding of its satirical nature. The author and publisher disclaim any liability arising from the misinterpretation of this work as anything other than fiction. By reading this book, you acknowledge that you understand it's a work of fiction meant to entertain and provoke thought, not to be taken as factual. Now, go ahead and enjoy the ride!

***

"Just because you don't take interest in politics, doesn't mean politics won't take interest in you!"
Pericles 495 BC - 429 BC.

Vote Young People, Vote!

The Prologue

"EMBRACE THE LIES! In Golf & Life, A Lie Is A Lie!"

Noah Philter was a legend in his own time—the kind of man whose stories were told and retold in every corner of the nation. In one famed incident, he swooped in to save a frail old woman and her treasured cat, Toto, from the ruthless swing of a developer's wrecking ball in downtown New York City. Under the ex-president's watchful eye, the demolition halted, the crowd cheered, and the media frenzy that followed cemented his status as a public hero. Yet, away from the limelight, Noah was a titan of industry, constructing an empire of luxurious hotels, sprawling casinos, and grand golf resorts.

But he grew restless, bored by his charmed life of wealth and luxury. This faded hero, who fired employees on reality TV, now dreamed of an even greater quest: making America great again.

The siren's call to run for President rang out, and the world (okay, part of it) clamored for his leadership. Philter smirked, "You do one good deed, and people forget what a degenerate you are."

Initially reluctant due to a busy schedule of cheating at golf tournaments, Noah was encouraged by his wise daughter Curvanka: "Think of the free publicity for our new Moscow hotel!"

Though President 44 rebuilt the country from the ruins left by the calamitous 43, Philter still knew he could do better. Boredom and ego motivated his run, interrupted only by court cases where the "Court Jester" relished in his second-favorite sport. That being said, there were legal battles. Challengers during the 2016 primaries proved mere tests; each swatted away with crass insults. The fawning press became his helpers, eating from his tiny palm. Lying came naturally—"he was worth $10 billion, the best golfer to ever walk the planet," a smart and humble businessman perfectly suited for the presidency.

His crowning achievement was propagating the falsehood that the 44th president, born in America, was somehow an illegitimate Kenyan, all while concealing his unsavory familial secrets and origins.

When party elders threatened to reject his unorthodox campaign, Philter hissed back, "I'll just self-fund and run independently!" Panicking at the prospect of his hordes of fans splintering off, the GOP caved with the super senior Senator from Kansas, aka Glitch McDonnell's blessing: "Be our hero, Noah. Anyone's better than 44!"

Somehow, someway, the lying lout won the presidency in 2016. No plan, no platform, no experience—just hilarity and chaos ensuing for years to come.

As president, Philter found new boredom. Reading daily briefings? No thanks. The Oval Office from Monday through Tuesday? A drag. Constant public scrutiny of his lies? How rude!

After some "chopper talk," he retreated to his golf resorts, dragging the mobile White House with him to soak taxpayers for room, cart, and food fees. A "working vacation" in the purest sense, save for the embarrassing eighteen club championships Philter brazenly awarded himself. The most profitable venture to date! Setting the all-time presidential vacation record, even outdoing 43's absenteeism, Noah ran America from his golf cart until disaster struck in the form of a virus he shrugged off as "the sniffles."

Completely unprepared and unwilling to confront a genuine emergency, the incompetent President and his V.P. babbled and downplayed it all, abandoning their responsibilities like vermin deserting a doomed vessel. Noah did what he did best—pointed fingers and made empty boasts. But in his narcissistic delusions of presidential power, the seeds were planted for his current world of legal hurt.

Many people, smart people even, believed Noah's subconscious desire to be held accountable drove his lawless behavior. If he couldn't deal with leading, he'd make the courts his new arena, a return to his sporting roots of troublesome litigation.

Having lost re-election while leaving America ablaze, the GOP still incredibly found no better 2024 candidate than a disgraced, twice-impeached former president while embracing fascism and facing 88 felony charges.

And that's where our story begins: Philter's quest for redemption through tyranny. The opportunities abound: rebranding his regressive party, reviving his sham university, persecuting more immigrants, and launching a revolutionary new "healthcare" system. Chafing at the bit for retribution against his perceived enemies, he promises to be a dictator starting on day one—what a joy!

Touted by TOXic Friends News Media's disinformation apparatus, Noah galvanizes a fresh cohort of authoritarians, aspiring to transform his administration into outright tyranny. Behold Wallabie Richman, the founder and CEO of TOXic, at the forefront with Philter guiding a motley crew of unprincipled individuals who have resurfaced to partake in the spoils. Some fresh faces join remnants from the deplorable 43rd regime (a few red giants among them), all poised to adopt their chief's toxic principles and reprehensible behavior. So prepare yourself, dear reader. This darkly satirical prologue is but a small taste of what's to come in the dystopian main course that follows. But first, Philter needs to win just one more tournament.

Tee'd up and ready to go!

Contents

About The Author   1
About Characteristic 26   2
Acknowledgments   3
The Prologue   7
Chapter 1: Fred Philter (Narration)   1
Chapter 2   4
Chapter 3   14
Chapter 4   23
Chapter 5   26
Chapter 6 Fainting Goats & Fainting Judges   28
Chapter 7   36
Chapter 8   38
Afterword   48
Encyclopedia/Guidebook/Wiki For The Embrace Books Series.   51

Chapter 1: Fred Philter (Narration)

Everything old is new again, especially during each election cycle.

Like so many other teenagers, my sister Lova and I were completely consumed by social media. Instagram, TikTok, you name it—we were always posting, scrolling, and watching videos; our lives pretty much revolved around those apps and feeds.

That's when these accounts started popping up, exposing the seriously messed-up stuff happening at our dad's media company, TOXic Friends. Posts from people our age and families began to flood in, describing how the network was disseminating lies and hate, brainwashing their loved ones.

It was a total gut punch, realizing that the same company funding our privileged lifestyle was poisoning so many others. We were stuck with a sinking feeling—our dad was no innocent bystander in this disaster.

With Mom's connections in intelligence circles, we'd seen projections of where this malignant stuff could lead if it kept metastasizing. Yet, there was Dad, occasionally admitting regret over the Philter monster he'd helped unleash through the network.

"I never foresaw it reaching this point," he'd say, as if that absolved him from lighting the match. Hearing the man who once campaigned for Hillary feel remorseful about the forces he'd enabled with Philter was a mind-bending paradox.

But what could we do? We were just kids, collateral damage from Dad's reckless choices. Lova took it much harder, enraged by the injustice of it all. Me, I felt impotent. Ashamed that our family contributed to such poisonous propaganda. No filter could block out that harsh reality.

I'm Fred Richman, Lova's twin, and you're getting the unvarnished truth from me as the narrator of this story. Our father is Wallabie Richman, founder and kingpin of the TOXic Friends media empire. So, like it or not, our family's been inextricably intertwined with the roots of this catastrophic mess.

Despite all of Mom's teachings on the philosophical notion of "thrownness"—how we're thrown into absurd worlds beyond our control—making sense of the rapidly devolving situation around us was an immense struggle.

"Thrownness is our predicament of being propelled into circumstances predetermined by factors preceding our existence," Mom would explain in her existentialist way.

Yet here I am, an unwitting bystander thrown into this circus of democracy being decimated at Doral. Tension saturates the air as the boundaries between politics, business, and personal vendettas disintegrate. It perfectly encapsulates the Philter era, when grabbing power and wealth bulldozed over all other principles, and the sanctity of democratic norms was repeatedly desecrated.

I never chose this slimy legacy or the Republican Party's ethical rot to become my heritage. But the cosmic dice roll marooned me here, a privileged kid witnessing this sham circus unfold, yet utterly powerless to escape the thrownness of it all.

***

NOW, THE GOLF ANNOUNCERS TAKE US TO THE ACTION.

"Well, folks, I don't know what to make of the madness we've just witnessed over these past few days!"

Chip Shooter's baritone voice boomed over the hushed murmurs of the gallery. Positioned at the famed 5th hole of the Kruger-

Dunning Orange Slice Golf Classic at Doral, he gripped his microphone tightly, still trying to process the unbelievable scenes that had taken place. They played the back nine first. Why? Just because you only live once!

"I've covered my fair share of golf tournaments over the years, Chip, but I can say without a shred of doubt that this one will go down in the history books as the most farcical, outrageous display I've ever borne witness to."

Mookie Doakes shook his head slowly, removing his trademark visor to wipe a bead of sweat from his brow. The two veteran broadcasters had been running the gamut of emotions—from amusement to bafflement to outright disgust—as the events of this year's Classic spiraled into absurdity.

"You took the words right out of my mouth, partner. When we signed on to lend our voices to this event, I don't think either of us could have possibly imagined the pure, unrestrained madness that would unfold."

Chip adjusted his earpiece, still processing the avalanche of controversies. Multiple player outbursts, baffling scoring discrepancies, and perhaps most memorably, the constant specter of potential champion Noah Philter casting the very rules of golf aside with impunity.

"And at the center of this three-ring circus was none other than Noah Philter himself. A man who, let's be honest, has always had a somewhat...flexible relationship with the concepts of ethics and integrity on the course." Golf is a place where he doesn't even like his own lies!

A sarcastic snort escaped Mookie's lips as he stared down the immaculate fairway, shaking his head.

Chapter 2

"Well folks, after that last delay, it seems like our former champion Noah Philter has finally arrived," Chip announced from the commentary booth. "And he's got some company—is that the 'anti-gravity' Senator Jon Ronson now riding alongside him?"

Mookie furrowed his brow quizzically. "Did you say anti-gravity?"

"Yes, that's what my nephew refers to him as," Chip chuckled. "Funny, huh? With that stack of paperwork he's holding, it looks like they're combining business and golf today. Or maybe Ronson has just stopped in to see if he's in the running to be Philter's VP pick. Could be Noah just likes to show off his souped-up golf cart, too."

The broadcasters' banter was interrupted as Philter teed off, his shot arcing down the fairway of the 5th hole at Doral.

"We are off on the 5th, and if you can believe it, Noah Philter is already eight strokes ahead." Chip marveled. "The man is an absolute wizard on the course."

Mookie scoffed loudly. "A wizard of deception is more like it, Chip! I've never seen such blatant cheating, even among weekend hacks. On the last hole alone, he kicked his ball out of three separate bunkers."

"You're just jealous you've never won six club championships in a single day like Noah has," Chip retorted with a sly grin. "The man gets results, even if his methods are...unorthodox."

"Unorthodox?!" Mookie sputtered in disbelief. "That's one word for it. I have a few other choice words..."

His retort was cut off by the earth-shaking rumble of Philter's obnoxiously loud hot rod golf cart barreling down the cart path towards them. Ronson clung on for dear life in the passenger seat, his paperwork getting whipped about by the wind.

"Noah rolls by the credo, 'fastest cart, best lies!'" Chip quipped dryly, "It looks like Noah is making his way up the first cut of rough again to improve his lie. The man plays by his own rules!"

Philter spotted his ball and slammed on the cart's brakes, sending it into a dusty, tire-shredding powerslide directly towards an unsuspecting spectator seated on the nearby white picket fence provided as bleachers.

Chip: "Get a load of the seating provided for some VIPs. It's temporary white picket fences they installed on the last nine holes for their comfort. It's for all those who were in the administration or government who flip-flopped on their take regarding all the crazy illegal activity Philter has committed, most right there in plain sight. Glitch, Barr, Kevin McCutie, the New Hampshire Governor, and don't forget Lady G from South Carolina—the list goes on. They've actually run out of space in these special seats. When asked if their seats were comfortable, they said, 'Thank you; we'd be happy to sit here as long as this tournament goes.'"

"Oh no! Heads up, Glitch McDonnell! Move your bones!" Mookie yelled in warning.

But the Senator had no time to react before the careening golf cart plowed right over him, its massive tires leaving deep tread marks across the man's crumpled suit.

"Yeesh, that's gonna leave a mark," Chip winced.

"You've got to be kidding me," Mookie seethed, shaking his head. "Poor Glitch looks like roadkill out there!"

The camera panned over to the motionless form of Glitch McDonnell lying in the rough, showing no signs of life. Philter hopped out of the cart and took a few practice swings, his expression one of total indifference to the human speed bump he'd just flattened.

"Wait, what's this?" Chip said, his eyes going wide. "Glitch is... regaining his footing? How is he possibly standing after that?"

To the broadcasters' astonishment, the disheveled man slowly picked himself up off the turf and began hobbling in an almost trance-like state back towards the provided seating.

"I'll be damned," Mookie muttered under his breath. "There he goes, trudging right back like nothing happened!"

Glitch collapsed back into his front-row seat, his suit in tatters and streaked with tire marks. With a pained grunt and broken glasses, he lifted his gaze towards Senator Ronson and gave a weak nod.

"I'll do anything... for the party," he wheezed.

Ronson simply nodded back, stone-faced.

Mookie and Chip exchanged a look of utter bewilderment.

"Did...did he just say what I think he said?" Chip sputtered. "What party could he possibly be referring to?"

"Your guess is as good as mine, Chip," Mookie replied, his voice flat with disbelief. "But one thing's for sure: we haven't seen shameless pandering like this since the last election!"

Chip could only shake his head. "No kidding. Stay tuned, folks; this Philter freak show just continues to get weirder and weirder!"

* * *

STRAWBERRY FIELDS & JUDGES FOREVER.

"Well folks, we were supposed to be heading into the final stretch of this tournament today," Chip Shooter's voice rang out over the broadcast. "But in a development that will surprise absolutely no one at this point, it appears the proceedings could be delayed. Again."

Cameras panned across Doral's sun-drenched grounds, a faint exhaust and dirt vortex swirling. From that hazy center emerged Noah Philter, trailed by his omnipresent private beverage and pie cart.

The unassuming cart was manned by a smiling attendant, Trovie, dishing out Philter's admitted weakness: fresh strawberry pie. His cravings for the fruity treat bordered on addiction, so much so that he'd had strawberry fields planted around Doral to supply his compulsive snacking. The cart's tins brimmed with lattice-topped indulgences baked from those very berries harvested through free labor provided by Doral's membership— long story. Pulling up beside the pie cart rumbled another vehicle—the "Finger in the Wind" public relations golf cart. This roving social media command center allowed Philter to broadcast his every lie instantly (he somehow always has the best lie of the course and the most damaging lie of the course), thoughts, and actions to the world. As it drew near, the unmistakable opening beats of a Taylor Swift pop anthem began thumping from its speakers. A look of childlike glee spread across Noah Philter's face. His eyes lit up, and his feet started tapping involuntarily into the infectious rhythm.

Before anyone could process what was happening, Philter launched into an exaggerated dance routine straight out of a music video. He twirled and shimmied between shots, throwing in some pelvic thrusts and hair flips for extra flair. His entourage of yes-men dutifully mimicked the moves behind him in a scene that could only be described as pure, unmitigated cringe.

"He's got moves like Jagger," Chip remarked with a chuckle. "Or should I say, more like those infamous dance moves Elaine broke out on Seinfeld?"

Trovie, the ever-present pie cart attendant, gamely tried to keep from busting out in laughter.

The broadcasters, Chip and Mookie, could only look on in stunned silence, their professional demeanors slipping as they struggled to stifle bemused chuckles. Mookie finally regained his composure enough to offer some commentary.

"I'm not sure what we're witnessing here, folks, but it certainly explains all the 'Dancing with the MAGA Stars' rumors that have been swirling," he managed between suppressed laughs. To witness Philter dancing in between shots to this music was something you absolutely could not unsee. It was a spectacle that seared itself into the brains of all who beheld it, like a surreal fever dream. Chip remarks that after all this, I like watching golf about 20% less!

"That's right, Chip," his co-commentator, Mookie Doakes, chimed in with a resigned sigh. "The eyes of the golfing world are all on Doral as we witness, for the sixth consecutive day, mind you, Philter's dog-and-pony show masquerading as a prestigious tournament."

Mookie nodded, taking a sip of water before continuing his commentary. "That whole Philter fiasco was a ridiculous mess. I didn't even get back to my hotel until late last night. I finally made it to my room, but then there was this massive rumbling."

He shook his head in disbelief. "Next thing I know, the ground just opens up—a sinkhole the size of an Olympic pool had formed right in the parking lot! It swallowed up a bunch of cars, including my rental."

Chip let out a low whistle. "A massive sinkhole opened up at your hotel. Now I've heard everything. Did you at least get the insurance option on that rental car?"

Mookie shot him an unamused look. "Very funny. No, I didn't, and now my clubs are gone too. I had to call an Uber just to get here."

Chip chuckled. "Rough luck, my friend. But I suppose that's a good transition to get us back to the actual tournament...if we can even call this farcical event that anymore."

He gestured out to the grounds where Philter's circus was still unfolding. "It seems our ringmaster has cooked up another ridiculous delay tactic while you were gone..."

As the two broadcasters took a breath, the rumbling roar of an approaching cart grew louder, and Swift's sugary vocals were now clearly audible over the engine.

The camera cuts to Noah Philter waving over two improbable caddie companions, Justice Robertson and Judge Irleen, the Supreme Court jurists now seemingly doubling as the former president's obsequious bagmen.

Philter greeted the jurists with an air of contrived urgency, saying, "John, Irleen (dressed in 'caddie' robes')...I'm relieved you've caught up," while casting exaggeratedly surreptitious glances around. "I'm afraid I'm having one of my...uh...let's call it a bad hair day brought on by this dreadful humidity."

Justice Robertson gave a solemn nod of understanding. "Say no more, sir. A bad hair day constitutes a legitimate environmental hazard per Section 6.2 of the official rulebook as you, yourself, decreed it."

Philter returned the gesture with equal gravitas. "Which is why I'll need one of you to officially delay things until my hair and I are both camera-ready. The optics, you understand."

Without hesitation, Judge Irleen produced a Sharpie marker. "Consider it decreed, Mr. Philter. I'll get right on formalizing this delay."

As Robertson and Irleen pored over the rulebook with flattering devotion, their colleague Justice Clary Thompson,

Philter's playing partner for the final round, looked on with mounting outrage. He marched over, his face reddening.

"Just a minute here!" Thompson sputtered indignantly. "Philter has appointed you two as tournament officials as well as his personal caddies? And now you're decreeing farcical delays at his whim? This is an outright violation of the rules and ethics of the game." "For shame".

The two officials exchanged a sheepish glance before nodding in unison. "By the power vested in us as your impartial rules officials," Robertson intoned, "we are hereby delaying the proceedings until...Mr. Philter has had sufficient time to tend to his hair."

A raucous ovation erupted from the sidelines, where a gaggle of sycophants seated on a white picket fence cheered and clapped with unrestrained glee.

"You hear that uproarious ovation, Mookie?" Chip said, his voice dripping with disdain. "Why, it's the deafening chorus of democracy dying a thousand cheers! That's the sound of the 'Trauncy' crowd eating up every undemocratic delay Philter can dish out."

Mookie scowled as the camera panned across the clapping throng of obsequious supporters—Glitch McDonnell, Barr Billy, Kevin McCutie, the New Hampshire Governor, Ted 'Marco' Ruse, and Lady G from South Carolina, among them.

"It's like a live taping of the Underminers at this point," Mookie groused. "Look at them, Chip—they're absolutely salivating at every ethics violation!"

Indeed, the sycophants seemed utterly enthralled, grinning widely as they clapped and cheered for Philter's blatant abuses of power.

"The man's a visionary!" Glitch hollered, his suit still bearing the tire marks from an earlier cart incident. "Only a true patriot would have the foresight to delay a tournament for the good of his hair!"

"Let us praise those crafting the regulations!" Barr Billy bellowed in agreement. "I shall endorse any action undertaken for the sake of our revered commander!"

"Yes, yes, the humidity is simply unacceptable for governing the free world!" Ted 'Marco' chimed in obsequiously. "A wise delay indeed!"

In the midst of the fawning cacophony, a flustered Jeff Underwood came rushing over to the broadcast booth, mopping sweat from his brow.

"Chip, Mookie, we're getting a lot of... well, let's call them notes of concern that your commentary is 'again' veering away from the tournament itself," the beleaguered producer fretted. "The sponsor would appreciate it if you could stick to the approved talking points going forward."

Chip looked at him incredulously. "Notes of concern? Why, Jeff, we're just calling it as we see it—this tournament has been one delayed disgrace after another. If the truth happens to veer away from the approved script, that's hardly our fault now, is it?" As the cameras continued rolling, capturing every farcical beat of the ongoing circus, it became increasingly clear that this event had devolved into something much larger than a mere golf tournament. This was a grand theatrical production—an absurdist satire playing out in real-time, with the very future of rules and ethics hanging in the balance.

Chapter 3

Serving as an omniscient voice in this prequel, I, Fred Richman, will offer you a few insights and context amidst the exchanges between Chip and Mookie, lending perspective as our family has had a rather intertwined role in the cause of all this chaos. Even with our mother's profound wisdom about the idea of "thrownness"—being thrown into an absurd world—we still struggled to make sense of the ridiculous situation unfolding around us.

"The concept of 'thrownness' encapsulates how individuals find themselves propelled into situations beyond their influence, their paths predetermined by elements that predate their very

being." As I bear witness to the mockery of democratic institutions unfolding at Doral, I cannot escape the feeling that I am but a bystander to the unchosen milieu I was thrown into.

The air was thick with tension and anticipation as the lines between politics, business, and personal interests became increasingly blurred. It was a scene that encapsulated the very essence of the Philter era—a time when the pursuit of power and influence knew no boundaries and the sanctity of democratic institutions was cast aside in favor of personal ambition.

I did not choose the moral morass that has now become my family's legacy or the ethical rot festering within the heart of the Republican movement. And yet, by the cosmic roll of the dice, here I am, granted the privileged vantage point to narrate this sham comeback circus but utterly powerless to extricate myself from its thrownness. At first glance, the shrouded 10-story edifice next door to Philter's National Doral Miami resort appeared to be an ordinary building undergoing fumigation. The scaffolding, construction crews, and insect control tent gave the appearance of routine pest remediation.

But those familiar with the machinations surrounding Philter's sham comeback bid recognized the ominous reality— this was ground zero for a brazen rebranding of American democracy itself.

Originally intended to house the grandiose presidential ambitions of Florida Governor "Boots" before his campaign flamed out faster than former poster boy Shcott 'Moon' Walker's attempt, the vacant tower had been covertly repurposed. Unbeknownst to the public, on Mr.'s orders, it was now the new home of the Republican National Committee headquarters, but for how long?

The GOP had seeded its control to become Philter's personalized amen corner and institutional rubber stamp, all housed on premises he could closely monitor.

In a move deplored by democratic purists as the death knell for judicial independence, several conservative Supreme Court justices had also taken up clandestine residence in a nearby Doral Villa. They positioned themselves to quickly approve any order Philter issued and to meet any of his other needs.

While oblivious onlookers assumed the shrouded tower was being tented for termites as Acme Extermination was emblazoned on the fabric, Jerkvanka Branding operatives were hard at work behind those muslin curtains. Erecting the grotesque centerpiece of Philter's rebranding—a 45-foot effigy of the man himself, arms outstretched in a messianic pose. Under this unsettling statue, the new moniker replaced any last remnants of the GOP's iconography.

Though still under wraps, this rebranding, so fresh that the sign crane is there, was rapidly taking shape as a fait accompli, implemented with Philter's trademark disregard for democratic decorum or legal adjudication of his conduct. Speaking of rebranding, Jerkvanka Branding is also hard at work, shall we say, updating the old family real estate university! Stay tuned on that one.

Any whistleblowers reckless enough to object were swiftly exiled to improvised backwater positions (think resort work) on the resort's fringes. The remaining sycophants cheered each encroachment, their zealotry calcifying.

So, while the Doral grounds maintained a facade of sun-soaked tranquility, a circus of democratic perversion was unfolding behind the curtains. The final un-razing would mark nothing less than the debut of Philter's authoritarian ambitions writ large.

* * *

The broadcasters, Chip and Mookie, watched on in stunned amazement as a truly surreal scene played out before them on the pristine fairways of Doral. In what could only be interpreted as a cryptic foreshadowing of rebranding efforts yet to be unveiled, a massive ostrich seemed to be relentlessly pursuing a screaming man across the meticulously manicured grass.

"Good heavens, who is that fleeing for his life?" Chip exclaimed, squinting to make out the hapless figure. "And more importantly...what in blazes is that ornery, overgrown fowl doing loose on this impeccable golf course?"

Mookie's eyes widened as the pieces fell into place. "Wait one second. If I'm not mistaken, that's former Senator O'Josh Haulinas being chased by what appears to be some sort of avian mascot?"

Indeed, the disheveled and panicked Haulinas was sprinting wildly, his expensive suit askew, as he dodged golf carts and waved his arms in sheer terror. In dogged pursuit, with an unmistakable aura of menace, waddled an enormous ostrich, its beady eyes locked on the terrified target.

"I don't think I've ever witnessed anything quite so bizarre in all my years covering this sport," Chip admitted, dumbfounded. "We're now headed into day six of what was supposed to be a simple two-day tournament featuring politicians and corporate sponsors, and I can only assume whoever else the ringmaster Noah Philter wished to personally humiliate on this stage. It's devolved into an absolute circus!"

Mookie could only nod as the chase reached feverish intensity, the ostrich's powerful legs closing the gap. "You took the words right out of my mouth, Chip. I still can't fathom how Philter managed to secure special exemptions for legendary players like Jack and Gary just so he could publicly embarrass them and inflate his already insatiable ego."

Shaking his head, Chip tried to steer the conversation back to the tournament itself as Haulinas tripped over a bunker lip, barely evading the snapping beak of the enraged ostrich.

"An absolute disgrace to the game. And now this three-ring fiasco culminates with the farcical championship match between the self-proclaimed 'Golfer in Cheat' Noah Philter and Judge Clary Thompson, the former college standout turned ethically compromised Supreme Court judge."

"That's right." Mookie's voice dripped with disdain. "Though from what I've heard through the grapevine, Clary's own path to the finals has been riddled with impropriety. I wouldn't put it past Philter's people to have maneuvered some backroom dealings to get their player this far."

In the distance, a conservative justice could be seen driving a riding mower across a sidehill, having apparently been conscripted into groundskeeping duties in Philter's anti-immigrant staff purge.

"Speaking of backroom dealings, did you catch a glimpse of Justice Bavanaugh over there operating that mower?" Chip pointed it out with obvious disdain. "With Philter's constant xenophobic rhetoric about immigrant workers, he's somehow scared off all his remaining course staff!"

Mookie scowled at the absurd sight. "Utterly unbelievable. So now he has to strong-arm his ideological allies on the Supreme Court into basically serving as his personal grounds crew just to keep this farcical tournament grinding along. It's a perfect encapsulation of how detached from reality this guy truly is."

Mookie sighed as the ostrich finally cornered the cowering Haulinas. "You're absolutely right, Chip. This final match is sure to be rife with more outrageous cheating controversies. With the way Philter conducts himself, rank dishonor and unrepentant ethical sacrifice are basically pre-requisites at this point." He shook his head, watching the hapless senator plead for his life against the ornery bird's snapping beak. "In this supposed gentlemanly game, players are expected to 'embrace their lie'—to accept and play through the difficult circumstances their ball settles in, no matter how unfair or unlucky."

Chip nodded slowly. "And yet, for a man who has embraced dishonesty as a way of life, even the smallest fib is never good enough. Embracing the lie is practically an ideology for Noah Philter."

"Precisely," Mookie agreed, realization dawning. "Which is why I now see this entire farcical event for what it truly is—the opening gambit in Philter's pathological pursuit to fully normalize the 'embracing of lies' across all levels of society."

He let out a rueful chuckle. "In golf, failing to 'embrace your lie' earns you a penalty. But for Philter, it's quite the opposite—he's made an entire career profiting off retelling, embellishing, and fully leaning into any untruth or deception that serves his interests in the moment."

Chip's expression turned grave. "You're right; this spectacle is just the prequel—the opening tee shot into the deep ethical rough if you will. I fear Philter is positioning this as ground zero for nothing less than the widespread normalization of dishonesty as a societal virtue."

The broadcasters lapsed into an uneasy silence as Haulinas's shrill cries of terror echoed across the grounds. If their intuition proved correct, this farcical tournament would indeed be a harbinger—the leading edge of a much more sinister ideological storm Philter was scheming to unleash. For someone who had become infamous for his own trail of dangerous lies, the former president now seemed determined to raise the bar for dishonor and deception to unprecedented new heights. And this glorified hate-watch of a spectacle clearly represented just the first insidious steps towards fully "embracing the lie" as a nationwide ethical virus. Everyone brace yourselves, folks—this one is shaping up to be a real doozy!"

* * *

Chip sighed as he surveyed the scene unfolding around them. "You know, Mookie, the more I learn about how this entire tournament came together, the more bizarrely convoluted it all gets."

He shook his head slowly. "Apparently, Philter had some underlying motives beyond just ego-stroking when he decided to move the entire Republican National Committee headquarters right next door to his championship course."

Mookie arched an eyebrow. "Oh really? Do elaborate, Chip. Though I can't say I'm surprised to hear there's even more shadiness going on behind the scenes of this fiasco."

"Well, from what I've heard through the grapevine, part of Philter's reasoning was to essentially have the compromised conservative Supreme Court justices take up residence right on the premises," Chip explained gravely.

"So, he could have a captive workforce to do his bidding on and off the course?" Mookie scoffed. "That's some next-level manipulation and coercion right there."

Chip nodded. "Exactly. With their living quarters situated on Philter's property, these justices are basically at his beck and call now. Whether it's mowing greens, raking bunkers, or I shudder to think what other unsavory tasks he might demand of them."

"A smart strategic move; I'll give the old snake that much," Mookie admitted grudgingly. "Keeping those, he's got compromised right under his thumb and ironclad control. Though also utterly unethical and likely blatantly illegal."

"When has something as trivial as ethics or legality ever stopped Noah Philter, though?"

Chip countered with a mirthless chuckle. "This is a man who's been impeached twice and is currently facing a staggering 88 charges across four separate cases. Rules and norms have never applied to the self-proclaimed Stable Genius."

Mookie nodded ruefully. "True that. At this point, I don't think anything could possibly surprise me in terms of Philter's boundless willingness to shamelessly consolidate power and punish anyone who doesn't obey his deranged, ego-driven whims."

There was a momentary pause as the two broadcasters reflected on the overwhelming corruption laid bare by this tournament.

"It's a true disgrace to the sanctity of the game we both love," Chip said at last, his voice heavy with dismay. "This entire Philter-hosted debacle has stripped away any veil of plausible deniability. The rampant cheating, cronyism, and toxic ego that seem to fuel his entire being are on full display for all to see."

"A black eye on the sport for sure," Mookie agreed somberly. "But I guess that's just par for the course with this perpetual Golfer in Cheat firmly at the center of it all. Better buckle up, folks; I've got an unsettling feeling the worst of Philter's unethical indignities is still yet to come."

As the two broadcasters exchanged a weary look, the groan of golf carts signaled that another ludicrous episode was about to unfold on the farcical stage of Philter's creation. This time, any trace of amusement had been replaced by dread, for they could no longer delude themselves about the true depths of depravity their sport had sunk to.

Chapter 4

The broadcasters had barely settled in when Mookie noticed movement out of the corner of his eye. Leaning in, he muttered, "Hey Chip, we've got company."

Chip followed his gaze to see a flustered young man in an ill-fitting suit rushing toward their booth, his face flushed with consternation. As he approached, his anxious eyes darted between them.

"Excuse me, gentlemen?" he sputtered. "Jeff Underwood, assistant sports producer. We've got some...complaints about your banter."

Mookie scoffed loudly. "Complaints? Some viewers bent out of shape over our honest commentary on this dumpster fire?"

Chip held up a placating hand. "Let's hear him out. What's the issue, Mr. Underwood?"

Underwood swallowed nervously. "Well, there's been blowback that you've both been a bit too...candidly criticizing Mr. Philter's approach today."

"You're kidding?" Mookie's eyes widened. "We're supposed to ignore Philter's blatant cheating and unethical behavior?"

"I'll remind you we have ironclad contracts allowing unvarnished commentary without censorship," Chip stated firmly.

"Of course, of course!" Underwood said it quickly. "But with leadership away, I've gotten heat from sponsors about reining you in..."

Mookie cut him off. "We're respected voices who call it as we see it, feathers be damned."

"If the audience has issues with us exposing violations, that's for them to take up with a therapist," Chip added disdainfully.

Underwood's shoulders slumped as his case crumbled. "I...informed them about your contracts. And with leadership secluded, I'm the only decision-maker left."

Mookie studied him carefully. "So, you're not muzzling our assessments?"

To his surprise, Underwood shook his head. "Actually...I agree with your stance. I'm a free speech absolutist."

Chip raised an eyebrow. "Is that right? Well, we have your blessing to proceed."

"Precisely," Underwood nodded. "Let the cameras roll uninterrupted. Que sera, sera—the audience can change the channel if needed."

A grin spread across Mookie's face as he realized they'd won an ally. "Baby, you're speaking my language! Count on us, exposing every lapse we see."

Underwood nodded, satisfied, and departed. The broadcasters watched him go in silence.

"Well, I'll be," Chip said at last. "I wasn't expecting our free speech plea to win him over so easily."

"Hey, I'm not questioning it!" Mookie chuckled. "We've got the green light for brutally honest commentary without filters."

Chip joined the laughter, shaking his head. "With Philter's reckless disregard for ethics out there, he'll give us plenty of material."

As their mirth subsided, they exchanged a sober look—a silent acknowledgment of their new role as ethical watchdogs over this farce. A heavy burden, but one they were determined to uphold with integrity, no matter whose feathers got ruffled.

They realized the true depths of moral decay this tournament represented. Their role transcended mere sportscasting into upholding the fundamental values their beloved game had lost. They were the lone voices striving to expose the rampant erosion of sporting nobility.

Chapter 5

The 7th hole at National Travesty Resort was a brutal par-4, even in ideal conditions. But the relentless downpours of the past two weeks had transformed the meandering creek into a raging river, severely narrowing the landing area.

As Noah Philter, aka the 'big stick', stepped up to the tee box, a defiant smirk crept across his face. Despite holding a commanding lead in the tournament, he clearly wasn't going to let a little adversity deter him from attempting to obliterate the course record.

His opening drive sliced violently to the right, the ball disappearing into the turbulent waters with a defeated "plunk." Undaunted, Noah Philter reached into his bag and launched a second ball down the fairway, only for it to meet a similar watery demise.

By his third attempt, a look of consternation had replaced the earlier bravado. This tee shot at least found the short grass, but the ball came to rest precariously close to the river's edge.

Seizing the opportunity, Clary Thompson strode confidently to the tee box. His drive landed safely in the middle of the fairway, providing a legitimate look at the green. As he stepped back, he allowed himself a subtle nod of satisfaction.

Back in the rough, Noah was rapidly unraveling. His fourth ball plunged into the churning currents almost immediately after being struck. The fifth joined it shortly after, a vicious slice sending it on an arcing trajectory into the depths. A hush fell over the gallery as the realization set in after nearly squandering his entire complement of balls, Noah Philter would again reload from the tee box while incurring a crippling penalty. His once-commanding lead had evaporated in one calamitous meltdown.

For his part, Clary displayed a measured poise as he surveyed his second shot into the green. With a smooth, compact swing, Clary lofted an immaculate approach and watched it while clutching his pearls, saying, "Yes, some men wear pearls," which settled just a few feet from the cup.

As Noah Philter, aka the 'duck,' trudged back to the tee in a foul mood, launching another drive that found the fairway, the broadcasters could scarcely contain their astonishment at the sudden reversal of fortunes. Two holes left!

Chapter 6 Fainting Goats & Fainting Judges.

After that Fiasco, we now got this. The 8th green at the Kruger-Dunning Classic was a bizarre spectacle. Nearly two dozen shaggy goats grazed lazily across the pristine bentgrass as flustered Supreme Court Justice Ret Bavenaugh frantically tried herding the wayward flock away.

It was part of Noah Philter's controversial "co-op" program at Doral. Facing staffing shortages, Philter's scheme conscripted elite members like Bavenaugh into a program that was not unlike an indentured grounds crew service.

Watching from the booth, commentator Mookie couldn't believe his eyes. "Wait, is that really a top judge moonlighting as a goat herder?"

Chip grinned at his baffled partner. "It seems the grounds crew got creative with staffing this tournament."

The situation was an unintended consequence of Philter's harsh anti-immigrant rhetoric alienating Doral's skilled workforce, leaving them desperately short-staffed.

In a misguided bid to stay operational, Philter's team embodied his "America First" policy by employing livestock—actual goats—as supplemental groundskeepers. Philter even spun it positively, boasting about "creating jobs for American animals."

Realizing he was on camera, an exhausted Bavenaugh paused to awkwardly wave, his face flushed from the relentless Florida heat. His plight was worsened by Florida Governor Boots' draconian no-water-break law for outdoor crews. Clearly dehydrated, it seemed only a matter of time before heat exhaustion took its toll.

Mookie frowned as the struggling judge chased another wayward goat. "They just let these...livestock groundskeepers roam freely, munching the course before a major event."

"Philter's team is grasping at straws to stay operational," Chip replied with a rueful chuckle.

The ill-conceived goat idea was reportedly Derrick Philter's brainchild—a nepotism hire backfiring when they realized too late that these were no ordinary goats but a fainting breed that passes out from any perceived threat.

Suddenly, the growl of Philter's cart sent the herd freezing, ears perked. Bavenaugh frantically tried keeping the spooked goats from losing it but to no avail.

The entire flock immediately collapsed in comically stiff, paralyzed heaps around the flustered judge. Mookie could only gape, slack-jawed.

"Okay, seriously...what did I just witness? Don't tell me this is judicial workout programming!"

Chip laughed heartily. "Not quite, Mook! Those are fainting goats—bred to pass out from any perceived danger, basically. Quite the unconventional groundskeepers!"

As if on cue, Philter's cart came barreling through, scattering the prone herd as he leaned out, swatting the hapless goats with a wedge. One finally roused, bleating indignantly, before fleeing Bavenaugh. That's when catastrophe struck. Overcome by heat exhaustion and dehydration, Judge Bavenaugh suddenly stumbled and collapsed onto the grass in a sickening crumple, fainting from the draconian policy's toll.

The cameras cut away, but Mookie and Chip knew this went far beyond a simple stunt gone awry.

Mookie shook his head. "You know, Chip, I'd say this whole fiasco perfectly exemplifies how Philter's rhetoric backfired spectacularly. They're so desperate that they've resorted to using actual livestock on the grounds. And now their draconian policies are putting people's health at grave risk."

Chip nodded thoughtfully. "A misguided, unproductive stance has gone completely off the rails. You'd think basic human decency would be wiser than pandering to one's base."

As the commotion continued below, Mookie leaned forward.

"I think we're witnessing the perfect storm of poor leadership, xenophobic rhetoric, and callous disregard for welfare—happening right before our eyes. Philter's team is spinning this as an 'America First' success, but really, they're just trying to distract from their own glaring mistakes with more pandering."

Mookie added solemnly, "And while we're on glaring mistakes, let's not forget Philter's catastrophic virus mishandling that cost my longtime golf buddy his life after taking 'promoted' bogus horse meds. Making a bad situation catastrophic."

Shaking his head, Mookie, back to the present, watched as Bavenaugh's near-motionless body was carted off, the camera zooming in as he mouthed "water!"

Interlude

The United States has been shaped by continuous waves of immigration from diverse peoples seeking new opportunities, blending traditions, and contributing to economic growth despite challenges of integration and discrimination.

In one estimate, 98% of Americans are either immigrants or descendants of immigrants. Is any educated person truly surprised?

Immigration is arguably the single most defining characteristic of the United States. Since its very founding as a nation built by those seeking new lives and opportunities, the arrival of diverse peoples has shaped its trajectory and identity.

The early waves of immigrants, primarily from Europe, provided the labor that fueled the burgeoning nation's agricultural and industrial revolutions. They brought with them traditions, skills, and cultural practices, which blended and evolved into the American tapestry. While not without its challenges, this influx of people contributed significantly to the nation's economic growth and expansion.

The late 19th and early 20th centuries saw a shift in immigration patterns, with Southern and Eastern Europeans arriving in large numbers. This period also witnessed a rise in anti-immigration sentiment and discriminatory policies, reflecting anxieties about cultural change and economic competition. Despite these hurdles, immigrants continued to contribute to American society, enriching its cultural landscape and adding to its economic vitality.

The latter half of the 20th century witnessed another wave of immigration, this time predominantly from Latin America and Asia. This wave brought renewed cultural dynamism and economic contributions, further diversifying the American experience.

Throughout its history, the United States has grappled with the challenges of integrating new arrivals and balancing ideals of inclusivity with anxieties about cultural change. The story of immigration to the United States is one of continuous evolution, a testament to the resilience and adaptability of both the newcomers and the nation itself. This ongoing narrative stands as a potent reminder that American identity is not static but rather a dynamic process continuously shaped by the influx of new people, perspectives, and dreams.

End of Interlude

"Who knew the real punchline would be subjecting this championship to such an undignified spectacle? All because the former president would rather pander than take the simple, sensible step of hiring immigrant labor?"

* * *

The broadcast cut away to the sidelines, where an intense argument was happening between Derrick and Jon Philter Jr. The former President's sons were about to start squabbling as they fiercely debated who deserved credit for the weird idea of using fainting goats as groundskeepers.

"I'm telling you, this was my idea!" Derrick insisted, puffing out his chest. "Who else would have the genius to replace all those immigrant workers with good old American livestock?"

Jon scoffed at his brother's boast. "Your idea? Don't make me laugh. I remember suggesting we look into an all-American grounds crew after Dad's Bedminster place got in trouble for hiring illegals."

Derrick refused to back down. "Maybe you mentioned wanting American workers, but only I connected the dots to using four-legged Americans!"

Jon rolled his eyes dramatically. "Connecting dots? Please, you couldn't connect a number to bingo without someone holding your hand."

The insult was the final straw. Derrick's face turned red with anger, and he got right in Jon's face. "Say that again, and I'll show you who needs supervision!"

From the broadcast booth, Mookie cut in with a smirk. "It looks like the Philter family quarrel is already in full swing today!"

Beside him, Chip chuckled dryly. "Indeed, Mookie. Theu former President's sons are...debating who gets credit for today's unorthodox staffing decision."

As they watched, Jon shoved Derrick hard in the chest. His brother immediately shoved him back with even more force. The two started a childish pushing match right there on the grounds of the prestigious golf tournament.

The broadcasters laughed uproariously as the camera stayed on the squabbling Philter brothers.

Wiping a tear from his eye, Mookie chuckled. "Oh, they're really milking this for all it's worth, aren't they? And we still have a hole to go in the tournament!"

He shook his head in amusement and disbelief, watching as the infantile clash showed no signs of stopping. Derrick and Jon seemed determined to resolve their argument through juvenile shoving rather than a calm discussion.

"You know, it's almost sad," Mookie said. "To think one of those idiots actually wants to follow in his dad's footsteps all the way to the White House. I don't think even TOXic news would touch that story."

Chip let out a hearty laugh at his partner's quip. Watching the Philter brothers devolve into a pathetic shoe-shoving match certainly painted another embarrassing picture of the family's legacy.

"Well, I suppose we should just be grateful this ridiculous display is almost over," he said, straightening his tie. "One more hole after this childish exhibition, and we're out of here, Mook. Small blessings, eh?"

Mookie nodded, transfixed by the former President's bickering sons upholding their father's petty, boorish reputation.

"You know, now that you mention it...," Mookie said thoughtfully. "Rumor has it; those two con artists were trying to find investors at this very event for some new shady healthcare business scheme of theirs."

Chip's brow furrowed curiously. "Oh? Do tell."

"Get this—the name of their company. 'The Next Mark Bros. Despicable VC Firm' or some nonsense like that," Mookie said with a derisive snort. "They're basically broadcasting their ethics with a name like that."

He shook his head, clearly disgusted by the Philter boys' shameless hustling. It is surprising who they inherited their conman genes from.

Chapter 7

The fairway of the 9th hole transformed into a scene of protest as Mookie and Chip watched with wide eyes. A group of former officials who had served in Noah Philter's administration lined up defiantly, suit jackets removed.

"Would you look at that?" Mookie exclaimed. "We know Philter's got himself a cheering squad following him around, but that protesting group outnumbers them big time!"

Raucous cheers echoed from Philter's ardent supporters seated atop the pristine white picket fences ringing the hole. However, the broadcasters' attention was drawn to the larger opposition contingent assembling on the fairway itself.

Chip squinted at the sizable group. "If I'm not mistaken, those are former Philter administration officials! I see the ex-Secretary of State, ambassadors, even the old Vice President."

"You're right," Mookie said with a low whistle. "And check it out—the entire January 6th committee is here too!"

The mismatched crew of one-time Philter confidants made for a striking scene, flanked by prominent Republicans and retired generals. The highest-ranking former government figures grimly lined the fairway, a stark contrast to Philter's rambunctious fans.

"Look at what they're doing!" Chip's eyes widened as the protesters shrugged off their jackets in choreographed unison. "Good lord, they're spelling something with the lining!"

Held aloft, the inverted suit jackets boldly displayed a crimson message: 'NOAHS NOT FIT FOR OFFICE.'

The broadcasters exchanged an incredulous glance, stunned and momentarily silent by the brazen rebuke from Philter's inner circle. But their shock was short-lived as FL. Governor Boots' State Sentrys, part of Boots' 25-person security force (he's afraid of mice) he travels with (he's at Doral sniffing around about being V.P.), quickly swarmed the protesters.

"Well, so much for that statement," Mookie said sarcastically as the jackets were confiscated. "Boots is so well-liked, he has to have his own personal army keep dissenters in line, and I, too, think he also wanted to be the nominee."

Chip shook his head. "Those who know him best sure don't mince words about Philter's fitness for office. Though their protest was short-lived thanks to the governor's hired muscle."

Chapter 8

The Final Hole

Mookie discreetly checked his notes as he and Chip watched the hulking figures of Noah Philter and Clary make their way toward the final tee box, unaware their microphones were still live.

"Well, we're finally winding down to the end of this surreal spectacle," Mookie muttered, shaking his head. "Though with Philter involved, who knows what fresh indignities are in store for this finale."

Chip let out a weary sigh. "I'm just spent after this nonstop, shall we say, head-scratching activity. At least it'll be over soon enough."

There was a brief pause as Philter and Thompson appeared to be bickering over who had honors for the final tee shot. Mookie seized the opportunity.

"Speaking of being spent, where are you off to next after this circus?" he asked his broadcast partner. "I heard a rumor you were slated for something called the 'Emasculated Senator Open' down in Houston."

Chip's eyes widened in recognition. "Oh yeah, that ultra-conservative glamor-fest hosted by Ted himself. It was supposed to be the first of five of these niche tournaments I regrettably signed on to cover for an obscene amount of guaranteed money."

He shook his head ruefully. "But that plan got washed out—literally. From what I've heard, Houston got absolutely pummeled with about two feet of rainfall in a single day recently. Entire neighborhoods turned into raging rivers. The planned tournament site is still underwater."

Realization dawned on Mookie's face. "Wait, you're talking about that same biblical storm system that rolled through here and basically created a water hazard smack dab in the middle of the seventh fairway, and I guess that rain could have caused the sinkhole that took my rental?"

Chip nodded grimly. "The very same. I thought watching Philter hack away from that newly formed 'river' was the peak of this event's absurdity. But it sounds like Houston took things to a whole new level of apocalyptic conditions."

A tense quietness descended upon them as they pondered the escalating devastating effects of ecological turmoil. Ultimately, Chip shattered the stillness with a humorless snicker.

"Well, at least our guaranteed contracts mean we're safe for now from being fired," he said. "You know the rules, though— talk about 'bikini waxed greens' on a hot mic like I did, and you're gone before you can say 'dimpled Orb.'"

Mookie couldn't help but snort out a laugh at that. "Some lines you just don't cross in this business, my friend. No matter how farcical the proceedings become."

Any further quips were cut off as a sudden commotion drew their attention back to the 9th tee box. There stood Clary, finally having settled the dispute over honors as he settled over his ball. Noah glowered disapprovingly nearby, no doubt itching to get this regrettable day over with. Mookie shot Chip a wry grin as he realized their mics were still live. Leaning in, he announced with his trademark flair:

"And dare we say, after all the madness we've witnessed, our plucky underdog Clary actually has a chance to pull off an upset for the ages here on the final hole!"

As Clary took his stance and the crowd hushed in anticipation, the two broadcasters could only shake their heads and prepare for one final descent into satirical absurdity. Though given everything they'd endured over the past few days, was there any spectacle too outrageous left to surprise them?

* * *

Noah Philter walked to the last hole, even though they both made par on the goat hole, he really hacked up the seventh and let Clary back in the tournament, but his temper was still flaring. But what really got him to the next level of anger was discovering that Thompson had taken the last slice of pie from his pie cart. His eyes blazed with anger as he confronted Clary, who was casually eating a fresh strawberry pie, seemingly unaware of the storm brewing.

"Those slices were mine, Clary!" Philter's voice boomed, his face redder than a ripe strawberry. "They had my name on them. You had no right to take them!"

Clary took a step back, his fork still in his mouth. "I thought since you'd already eaten the rest of the pie, Noah, I figured I'd grab a slice while you were struggling on the last hole. Plus, I picked strawberries yesterday as part of my golf membership duties. "Philter's face was twisted in outrage, his voice dripping with sarcasm. "So, you're a strawberry guy now? Well, let me tell you, Clary, on my course, with my strawberries and my pie cart, it's my right to eat all the pie that I want."

The air was tense, and the only sound was the sweet chirping of birds from atop the cart, a stark contrast to the dark humor unfolding before them. Clary couldn't help but crack a small smile, which only fueled Philter's anger. Philter's tone escalated, his words dripping with indignation as he teetered on the brink of a comical outburst. "Do you find amusement in this, Clary? Is my pie a source of humor for you?"

"Calm down, Noah," Clary said, trying to intervene. "We've got one hole left to play."

***

An Interlude

Since rights were mentioned.

"Equal rights for others do not mean less rights for you. It's not pie."

Author unknown.

***

Chip's voice carried a reverent hush as he addressed the viewers. "Well, folks, the Kruger-Dunning Orange Slice Golf Classic at Doral has arrived at its dramatic crescendo—the legendary 9th hole designed by the one and only Alister Treat Dye. A par three so utterly diabolical, it makes one question if 'Treat' was meant as some sort of sadistic double entendre."

"You can say that again, Chip," Mookie agreed with a grimace. "This hole is anything but a treat, especially with the challenging wind conditions we're experiencing."

The camera panned over the raised, undulated putting surface, completely obscured from the tee box by a massive crest in the layup area. Looming like a malevolent rise of earth, dividing the haves from the have-nots.

"Precisely, Mook," Chip intoned gravely. "The green complex is essentially a black box from the tee deck. Players have to hit blindly over that hill and let whatever Dye-abolical creations await sort out their fate."

Down on the tee box, the air was thick with tension. Judge Irleen frantically dug through Noah Philter's gaudy golf bag, her face etched with concern.

"Mr. President!" She pulled out a pristine blue Titleist ball and thrust it towards Noah. "This is a crisis situation—you're down to your last ball! It's one of the lucky blue ones your wife gave you before the tournament started. She made you promise to save these for when you really needed them."

Chip's sonorous tones dripped with melodramatic gravitas. "And need it he does, folks. After an absolutely calamitous performance on the hazard-riddled 7th hole, the former leader of the free world finds himself staring down the fairway of ultimate embarrassment here at the 9th tee box."

He paused for dramatic effect as Noah moved to the tee box, Clary Thompson looking at his options. Jon Ronson sat perched nearby on Philter's golf cart, seemingly oblivious to the surrounding circus as he pored over a sheaf of papers.

Mookie could only scoff at his broadcast partner's overblown commentary. "What, you mean more embarrassing than that audition for the Village People cover band he did in that 'patriotic' singlet outfit?"

Chip steadfastly ignored the jibe, his voice rising to a crescendo of hype. "This solitary blue sphere may be Noah Philter's last chance to etch his name into the pantheon of golf's honored icons! The pressure is insufferable; the stakes are stratospheric as he steps up. Live on the TOXic network..."

"It's just a dumb golf ball, Chip," Mookie deadpanned. "No need to be more dramatic than a Philter Steak commercial."

The former president's caddie extended the precious blue orb towards him again. "Make it count, Mr. President," she implored solemnly. "Your bride picked these out special for a moment like this."

Philter's gaze locked intensely onto Clary, his eyes narrowing as he seemed to be trying some sort of jet-eye mind trick on Clary. Beside him, Clary shifted impatiently from foot to foot.

Suddenly, in one furious motion, he stepped up and lashed at his ball. The hush was broken by a rustle of papers as Jon Ronson loudly rifled through his dossiers, clearly an assist to his new bestie. Clary's ball shot wildly off the heel of his club and skittered down into the thick strawberry patch guarding the left side of the hole. Oh, the irony. A blazing torrent of profanity erupted from Clary's lips as he watched his title hopes disappear into the brambles. Clary whipped his head around to glare at the a-hole, his jaw clenched in annoyance.

Chip could barely contain his delight at this fresh twist. In hushed, breathless tones, he proclaimed: "You can cut the tension with a sand wedge right now, folks. One ball left to autograph his legacy! The...Tangerine...Avenger...towering over his...Waterloo!"

"Oy vey, here we go," Mookie groaned, his voice dripping with droll sarcasm. "Someone get this boychik a fainting couch for when he busts a valve over a stupid golf ball."

With Clary still raging impotently, all eyes turned to Philter as he stepped over his solitary remaining sphere. Taking one final calming breath, he lashed out with every ounce of his being, his swing unleashing an absolutely titanic blast that sent the ball soaring massively skyward.

The broadcast crew craned their necks, straining to track its towering flight as it reached its zenith high among the scattered clouds.

"Wait for it...wait for it..." Mookie murmured in awe. "THERE IT IS! That ball is an absolute NUKE! It looks like it could be headed right for the cup!"

Chip could scarcely believe his eyes. "You're not kidding! If that finds the bottom of the jar, we could be witnessing Philter's 80th career hole-in-one. Though, at this point, I fear those are mere statistics to feed his ego." The camera pans back to the tee only to see Clary on the ground, clasping his chest. Noah was beside himself with giddy excitement as his majestic drive began its descent towards the hidden green, obscured by the menacing crest. Without warning, he sprang into his golf cart, Jon Ronson barely avoiding being thrown free as the former president slammed the accelerator.

The cart's tires spat out furious divots as Noah cackled with unrestrained glee, rapidly building speed as he cut a trench toward the base of the slope. Faint rumblings began to echo underfoot as his ball appeared to be striking the raised putting surface.

"Oh no..." Mookie's face drained of color as he realized Philter's intentions. "Don't tell me he's going to try and DRIVE up and over that hill to see where it finishes?!?"

But the former president only whooped with delight, cackling, "Jon, I think this is the beginning of a beautiful friendship!" as he showed his typical disregard for sanity or safety. The cart continued rapidly accelerating, aiming directly towards the precipice.

"THE HEAVENS PARTED AND THAT BALL COULD BE HOLE-BOUND!" Chip bellowed in disbelief. "But this madman is hurtling towards that hill to try and chase after it?!?"

"BRACE FOR IMPACT!" Mookie yelled, his voice edging towards panic. "THE TANGERINE TERROR IS ABOUT TO--"

He never got to finish his sentence. With the accelerator pegged, Philter's cart caught air off the steep slope's angle, sailing improbably over the crest before landing with a bone-jarring thud on the far side. A vast billow of dust and debris erupted into the air as if on cue. The rumblings underfoot rapidly escalated into a terrifying mini-earthquake, with the ground beginning to shake and heave all around them violently. Mookie could only gape in stunned horror.

"WHAT IN THE ACTUAL--?!?" He cried out. "PLEASE DON'T LET THIS BE HAPPENING!"

But it was. With a roar like the incoming apocalypse itself, a gaping sinkhole suddenly ruptured open in the area where the 9th green was located, swallowing the entire surface in a plume of dirt, grass, and chaos.

Philter's cart and its occupants disappeared from view in an instant, consumed by the abyss. A stunned hush fell over the scattered gallery as the dust finally settled, the area now marred by a vast, ragged pit where the green used to sit.

For several long moments, the scene was quiet, but the occasional dislodged clump of grass and dirt continued to patter into the depths below. Finally, one voice broke the bewildered silence.

It was Noah's former vice president and sidekick, Indy Penceadent, rushing to the precipice and peering over into the newly formed chasm with a look of disbelieving dismay. Shaking his head slowly, he remarked with a sardonic chuckle:

"Well, I'll be damned...Mother, Looks it's 'a-hole'!"

A hush enveloped the area as Penceadent's dark quip landed, the broadcast transitioning to stunned silence before a smattering of nervous applause rippled through the gallery. The shocking, calamitous final chapter of Philter's wildly entertaining comeback bid was now indelibly seared into the minds of all who witnessed it firsthand. For those only learning of it after the fact, the reports would surely read as satirical fiction rather than actual events. Adept at creating laws and norms, perhaps—but actively cheating death itself? For a man as skilled at evading consequences as Noah Philter, did nine lives truly exist?

And yet, this literal sinking act had transpired on the 9th hole—an ominous numerical portent for the farcical ethical Armageddon that was still to unfold across the nation. If such grotesque absurdities could manifest on this isolated golf course, what greater chaos could arise when bad-faith actors began leveraging their powers on a grander stage?

As the broadcast crew looked on in stunned bemusement, a smattering of papers came fluttering down to land at their feet. Senator Jon Ronson's "TOP SECRET" dossiers from the cart are now scattered in the aftermath.

The top page's partially obscured title seemed to declare "Project 2025" CLASSIFIED in bold lettering. Another sheet appeared to list a slate of "Alternate Electors" for the upcoming 2024 election.

Mookie and Chip exchanged an uneasy glance, their earlier lighthearted banter now feeling like a relic from a bygone era of blissful ignorance. For embedded within this scene of zany, slapstick mayhem, a darker omen had been inadvertently exposed.

Embrace the lies; it's Deja Vu all over again.

Vote. It's democracy or the dictator in waiting.

Afterword

An aside, "The mistake is to assume that rulers who came to power through institutions cannot change or destroy these very institutions, even when that is exactly what they have announced that they will do." And.. " Institutions do not protect themselves. They fall one after the other unless each is defended from the beginning. So, choose an institution you care about - a court, a newspaper, a law, a labor union—and take its side."

Timothy Snyder.

FRED, again.

"One last aside," I began, trying to convey urgency and determination. "This is crazy stuff, just a prequel to EMBRACE THE VIRUS, but it's all true, even though we're not old enough to vote yet."

I glanced at my sister Lova, who nodded encouragingly. "My sister and I are encouraging everybody to vote. My family, my dad specifically, and his company, TOXic, along with Noah, are flushing this country down the toilet for profit."

"We implore you to vote. Get your families to vote, get young people of all ages to vote, get older people to vote. Vote Blue, and if they can't stomach that, get them to skip a cycle. Our Republic is in the balance."

Lova stepped forward, her gaze resolute. "Within this prequel," she said, "there will be links or web addresses to pages that have easy-to-use, easy-to-share pledges. Fred and I will be taking these pledges and sharing them with as many families and friends as we can. The power of social media works two ways!"

I added, "We are peers; we want to vote. We want to take part in this great experiment, which is the United States. If this doesn't go right, this could be the last time our country votes in our lifetime."

Lova nodded solemnly. She understood the implications of what we were facing—a threat to the very foundation of our democracy. We had witnessed firsthand the machinations of our father's TOXic media empire and the insidious influence it wielded over public opinion.

As I spoke, my mind raced with the memories of the events that had unfolded before our eyes. The blatant disregard for ethics, the normalization of dishonesty at the farcical golf tournament, the whispers of a clandestine project to undermine the democratic process—all of it coalesced into a sense of urgency that fueled my impassioned plea.

I thought of the vacant tower looming over Philter's resort, a shrouded edifice that housed the very heart of the Republican National Committee, now under the ex-president's control. The proximity of the conservative Supreme Court justices, residing nearby for efficient rubberstamping of Philter's orders, sent a chill down my spine.

Yet, amidst the darkness, I found hope in the resilience of the American people. I believed in our collective power to shape our destiny and safeguard the principles upon which our nation was built.

"A confidential dossier that my mother shared with us, in relation to predictive analysis of where we are headed, also included the antidote for this, and that is it is up to us to be our own heroes and to own our future, and it starts with me, my sister (we will encourage as we are still too young to vote) and those just old enough to vote and beyond to take control of the future and vote as if everybody's molecules matter."

"VOTE."

I nodded. "Thank you," I said sincerely. "And we will see you in the main novel, EMBRACE THE VIRUSES. Or not!"

"We implore you to take action now. Our democracy is at a critical juncture, and your vote is vital. Encourage your families, friends, and peers to vote. Whether you're young or old, your voice matters. If voting Blue isn't an option, consider skipping a cycle, but do not stay silent. Our Republic is in the balance, and it is up to us to protect its future. Share the easy-to-use pledges and resources we'll provide, and use the power of social media to spread the word. Stand with us, take control of our future, and vote as if everyone's well-being depends on it—because it does. VOTE."

***

"The modern conservative is engaged in one of man's oldest exercises in moral philosophy; that is, the search for a superior moral justification for selfishness." John Kenneth Galbraith

***

ENCYCLOPEDIA/GUIDEBOOK/WIKI For the EMBRACE books series.

Viruses in the EMBRACE Novels

The EMBRACE novels explore various "viruses," both literal and figurative, that plague society:

- **Sporebourne Virusx:** This deadly pathogen emerges from the unsanitary conditions at Tangerine Medical University, where Inadequit Healthcare Systems develops its "Red Treatment." The virus contaminates the robotic workforce used in hospitals and represents the unintended consequences of unchecked ambition and prioritizing profit over safety. This item has its own listing; see.

- **Covid-19:** The novels highlight the disastrous mishandling of the Covid-19 pandemic in the United States, contrasting it with Australia's successful approach. Noah Philter's administration downplayed the threat, spread misinformation, and prioritized personal freedom over public health, leading to a devastating loss of life.

- **Greed:** Greed acts as a pervasive "virus," infecting characters like Wallabie Richman and the Philter brothers. Their relentless pursuit of wealth and power blinds them to ethical considerations and the well-being of others.

- **Fascism:** The novels depict fascism as an insidious "virus" slowly infiltrating society. Noah Philter, with his authoritarian tendencies and disdain for democratic norms, embodies this threat. The 1864 Monocle Party, with its antiquated values and emphasis on elite privilege, represents the culmination of this creeping fascism.

- **Lies and Dishonesty:** Lying as a Virus? Seems contagious. Noah Philter is a pathological liar, both on the golf course and in his personal and political life. He embodies the erosion of truth and integrity, embracing lies as a means to an end.

Sporebourne Virusx

The Sporebourne Virusx: A Preventable Endemic

The Sporebourne Virusx emerged from the unsanitary conditions of Tangerine Medical University, a repurposed real estate venture turned research facility for the Red Treatment and robotic assembly. Moldy food and decay were left unchecked, creating a breeding ground for the virus. Unknowingly, the Virusx clung to the robots being assembled by other robots, without human oversight, in a drive to maximize profits.

In the pursuit of profits, safety and hygiene protocols were ignored. The university's facilities were left in a state of disarray, with abandoned restaurants and food bars still containing petrified half-eaten meals. This created an environment where the Virusx could thrive.

The Red Treatment, developed at Tangerine, was pushed out at warp speed using an all-robot staff. The creators were so consumed by profit that they neglected biological safety, unleashing the Virusx on the world. The consequences of this disaster are still unfolding, but one thing is certain: the pursuit of profit over human life has consequences!

TOXic Friends News Media

TOXic Friends News Media (a fictionalized version of ? News) plays a central role in the spread of misinformation and the erosion of democratic norms in the EMBRACE novels. Founded by Wallabie Richman, TOXic prioritizes profit over truth, employing opinion hosts who deliberately stoke outrage and division to boost ratings.

The company's lawyers even admit, "Nobody believes them, nobody listens to them, it's just opinions," highlighting the cynical disregard for facts and the manipulation of viewers.

TOXic's Harmful Impact on America

The novels depict TOXic as a driving force behind several damaging trends in American society:

- **Rise of Noah Philter:** TOXic provides a platform for Philter's demagoguery and authoritarian rhetoric, helping him secure the presidency despite his blatant incompetence and disregard for democratic norms.

- **Mishandling of the COVID-19 Pandemic:** TOXic downplays the severity of the virus, promotes conspiracy theories, and undermines public health messaging, exacerbating the pandemic's impact in the United States.

- **Promotion of the "Rigged Election" Conspiracy:** TOXic relentlessly pushes the false narrative that the 2020 election was stolen from Philter, fueling distrust in democratic institutions and inciting violence.

- **Normalization of Lies and Disinformation:** TOXic's opinion hosts blur the lines between fact and fiction, conditioning viewers to accept unsubstantiated claims and reject legitimate sources of information.

- **Erosion of Trust in Media:** TOXic's blatant bias and manipulation undermine public trust in media as a whole, creating fertile ground for the spread of conspiracy theories and propaganda.

Internal Conflicts and Regret

Wallabie Richman, the founder of TOXic, experiences moments of guilt and regret over the monster he has helped create. He acknowledges the damage Philter has inflicted on America and expresses concern over the spread of misinformation.

However, these ethical qualms are often overshadowed by his ambition and desire for personal gain. His sons, Edgar and Oliver, further encourage his pursuit of profit, pushing him into increasingly risky ventures that prioritize financial success over moral considerations.

The Rise of TOXic Friends Global Media

Once upon a time, in a land where truth was supposed to matter, there lived a media empire that cared more about making a quick buck than telling it like it was. This empire was called TOXic Friends Global Media, and it was founded by a dude named Wallabie Richman, who had a great craving for money and power.

Wallabie saw an opportunity in 1996—a chance to create an "alternative facts" channel that would cater to the ultra-conservative crowd. All the other big news networks were too busy reporting actual news, so Wallabie figured he could swoop in and give the people what they really wanted: outrageous opinions and blatant misinformation!

At first, the mainstream media laughed off TOXic Friends as a joke. "An entire network dedicated to lies and nonsense? That'll never work!" they chuckled amongst themselves. But oh, how wrong they were. Before long, TOXic Friends had amassed a cult following of viewers who were hungry for someone to validate their worst prejudices on a daily basis.

The Cult of Outrageousness

What made TOXic Friends so wildly popular? Two words: opinion hosts. These were the real stars of the show, guys like Lucky Bile and Lean Mannity, whose entire job was to rant, rave, and misinform their audiences into an enraged frenzy.

These hosts were masters of mixing just enough truth with blatant lies to create a perfect Molotov cocktail of outrage, tailor-made for people who felt like their bigoted views were being ignored by the so-called "mainstream media." No topic was off-limits, whether it was demonizing minorities, pushing wild conspiracy theories, or just railing against anyone who didn't think exactly like them.

Of course, when these ranting ranters were called out for their nonsense, the lawyers at TOXic Friends would simply shrug and say, "Hey, nobody actually believes this stuff! It's just opinion, not news." As if that made it okay to pump millions of Americans full of blatant misinformation on a daily basis!

The Pandora's Box of Lies

With its motley crew of outrage addicts leading the charge, TOXic Friends soon became ground zero for some of the most damaging lies and conspiracy theories in modern American history. Whether it was downplaying the severity of the COVID-19 pandemic or relentlessly pushing the "rigged election" nonsense after Philter's 2020 loss, this network seemed determined to create an alternate reality where facts no longer mattered.

Their crowning achievement? Helping to elevate a reality TV host named Noah Philter all the way to the presidency despite his breathtaking incompetence and utter disregard for democratic norms. For four long years, TOXic Friends acted as Philter's personal propaganda machine, defending every indefensible action while demonizing his opponents and undermining faith in journalism itself. In the end, the network that had once been a punchline became a very real and dangerous threat to American democracy. By blurring the lines between news and entertainment, fact and fiction, TOXic Friends conditioned an entire generation of viewers to simply accept whatever outrageous falsehoods aligned with their preexisting beliefs.

The Punchline Becomes the Punisher

Now, in the aftermath of Philter's disastrous reign, the very people who enabled this descent into madness are trying to distance themselves from the monster they created. The Richman family hopes to move on and rebrand, secure in their billions earned through shameless greed and disregard for the truth.

But the damage has been done. The virus of misinformation that TOXic Friends unleashed has burrowed deep into the fabric of society, creating a deep-rooted distrust of credible sources and nurturing a culture of conspiracy theories. Rebuilding that trust and restoring truth to its rightful place may take decades of hard work—a stark reminder that profiting off lies and hatred has consequences that can ripple across generations.

Lova Persson Richman

Codename: The Cognizant One.

Profile:

To the conservative pundits of her father's TOXic Friends Global Media empire, Lova Persson Richman is viewed as that dreaded thing—a "woke" teen activist. Yet, at just 16 years old, this passionate truthteller has exhibited a social consciousness and moral maturity that far exceed her privileged upbringing. Born into wealth as the daughter of powerful media mogul Wallabie Richman, Lova's moral compass was forged by her profound bond with progressive mother Anneli. As Wallabie chased riches and influence, Anneli imbued Lova with values starkly contrasting her father's greed-fueled agenda. This dichotomy forced the young heroine to grapple with "thrownness"—the notion she didn't choose her circumstances.

Rather than succumbing to jadedness or complacency, Lova yearns to leverage her privilege and platform as a force for positive change. But she doesn't yet know how to create that impact in a world beset by daunting crises like climate change, social inequality, and endless conflicts.

The Clarion Call:

As Lova witnesses her father Wallabies' reckless investment in the shady Inadequit hospital chain and its risky RED Treatment, she becomes the lone voice urging him to confront the catastrophic consequences his actions could unleash. While her reckless stepbrothers cheer on Wallabies' schemes, Lova watches in disbelief as he ignores all ethical alarms—concerns also shared by her twin brother Fred.

Lova's profound empathy and consciousness, instilled by Anneli, compel her to wield her platform for activism. Her confidant Milo, potentially tied to the little-known KSI intelligence agency, provides crucial guidance.

The Burden of Awareness:

Yet, for all her convictions, Lova grapples with angst over the real impact she can create. These doubts are compounded by exposure to social media, which criticizes her father's media empire for spreading misinformation that has caused rifts in families and led many to recklessly ignore public safety.

These sobering realizations threaten to overwhelm Lova's youthful idealism at times. But her multi-faceted personality shines through quirks like being a polyglot fluent in five languages, with a friendly rivalry to surpass her race car driver friend's seven tongues. When traveling, Lova insists on exploring local communities incognito to authentically connect with diverse cultures.

Her creative writing and daring hobbies like free diving, paragliding, and hang gliding provide outlets for her adventurous spirit. From exclusive summer camps, Lova formed deep bonds with other affluent, primarily conservative teens who shared her concerns about the future.

The Heroine's Journey:

These friendships will prove vital as Lova confronts her greatest challenge: attempting to make Wallabie take responsibility for his unethical dealings, even if it disrupts the family itself. Her moral convictions, rooted in Anneli's wisdom, push Lova's courage to its limits. Can she overcome being born into unchecked greed and propaganda? Will her stepbrothers' misdeeds steer Wallabies' empire towards calamity?

Lova's emotional arc promises to be a roller coaster as she evolves from a passionate but uncertain teen activist into a resolute voice of reason and change. Yes, self-doubt will arise over her ability to create a tangible impact. However, Lova's empathetic rationality, fortified by her upbringing and diverse friends' perspectives, will ultimately overcome such trepidations. With each obstacle, her determination strengthens to forge a new legacy.

From her globetrotting adventures to her fierce independence, Lova emerges as a truly multi-dimensional, inspirational protagonist for a new generation. One who dares to use her privilege to speak truth to power rather than remain a complacent beneficiary of it. Prepare to be awed by her against-all-odds journey to awaken her father's moral conscience - and potentially catalyze the positive revolution the world needs.

Noah Philters' Dossier; The Twice Impeached Former President.

Origins of an improbable birthplace and rise to power.

After winning one of the earliest U.S. lotteries and putting their windfall into a trust fund, Noah Philter's parents forsook conventional life to join the Pasteur Institute's humanitarian calling—administering life-saving vaccines to underserved populations across Africa and Haiti. It was during this roving volunteer mission that fate, with its trademark warped humor, saw fit to bless the couple with their troublemaking progeny. Noah was conceived in the most inauspicious of circumstances— in the cramped, zinc-plated confines of a Quonset hut far more accustomed to sheltering medical supplies than conjugal bliss. His actual birthplace remained obfuscated as the family's journey home underwent delays at Ellis Island, where their documentation proving American citizenship was lost to the depths.

By the time formalities were finally resolved, Noah had already arrived, making his inglorious entrance with trademark brashness. The bewildered processing clerk simply designated the newborn's place of birth as "U.S. Territorial Waters," appending a skeptical asterisk to tacitly acknowledge the absurdity.

Through means that remain murky to this day, Noah eventually inherited the entirety of the Philter family's amplified lottery trust. This immense windfall would provide the seeds to germinate his ethically challenged real estate ventures, Tangerine Medical University, and its series of audacious offshoots like the Inadequit hospital chain.

The Twice-Impeached Purveyor of Viral Chaos

Today, the once wealthy heir stands accused of 88 charges across 4 cases—a cemented legacy as perhaps the most incompetent president in U.S. history by any objective measure.

A famous golf cheat who somehow "won" championships at his own courses despite having no competition, Philter's tenure will be remembered as an administration that unleashed a Pandora's Box of viruses upon the nation. After hijacking the GOP, he distorted it into his aristocracy-fetishizing "1864 Monocle Party," leading what was once the proud elephant party to the edge of the tar pits of irrelevance and historical obscurity. Yet despite two impeachments, he improbably secured the 2024 Republican nomination while deeply enmeshed in the alarming machinations of Project 2025, a subversive agenda to undermine democracy itself.

A Perfect Storm of Destructive Viral Releases Philter's presidency was a cataclysmic parade of viral releases, both literal and figurative. His rampant COVID misinformation fueled an uncontrolled wildfire that allowed the actual virus to spread unchecked. In a perverse display of profits over human costs, his Inadequit healthcare scheme perverts "freedom" into a viral vector for greed and moral bankruptcy with its ethically dubious treatments. Tangerine University's robotic Red Treatment embodied the anti-medical mindset of cutting corners on safety to indulge his worst theatrical impulses.

Even as he reveled in the tawdry moral squalor of the Stormy Sirens escort business, Philter concurrently became a mainstream voice, amplifying the creeping virus of fascism seeping through America's fabric. He contorted the GOP into an absurd aristocracy-fetishizing farce dubbed the 1864 Monocle Party, then cemented a conservative SCOTUS supermajority with the underhanded assistance of Sen. Glitch McDonnell—all to erode democratic norms and clear a path for authoritarianism.

On the existential issue of climate change, the former leader shamelessly mocked environmental concerns while doubling down on fossil fuel extraction, unleashing the viral spread of environmental degradation.

The Punchline's Irrelevance Embraced

Now facing a litany of charges, the fallen former king presides over the conservative movement's descent into the tar pits of irrelevance after inspiring the democracy-undermining agenda of Project 2025. After President #43 had already mortally wounded the GOP, Philter's unending cavalcade of failures, scandals, and viral releases has led what remained of the once-defiant elephant party to the very edge of the tar pits of historical obscurity, reduced to a flightless bird burying its head in delusion as American democracy erodes around it.

The narcissist who once craved attention at all costs has ultimately cemented his own infamy, with the conservative party's embarrassing devolution into a punchline as his satirical legacy, personifying democracy's downfall through an enthusiastic embrace of society's most destructive viruses—from COVID to greed, from extreme freedoms without regard for others to the insidious spread of fascism.

LIES

A line item that needs to be listed. Noah Philter made over 40,000 lies (and counting) during his tenure related to his 'role' as president, and that doesn't include lies to his wives, exes, or golf partners.

Wallabie Reuben Richman

Founder and CEO of TOXic Global Media

Profile:

Wallabie Reuben Richman, the 82-year-old head of the notoriously unscrupulous TOXic Friends Global Media conglomerate, personifies the age-old conflict between paternal love and an insatiable lust for power, wealth, and relevance. To his daughter Lova, he is both the doting father figure and the embodiment of unchecked corporate greed she has sworn to defy.

Once a man of modest means, Wallabies' uncompromising ambition propelled him to dizzying heights of success and outsized influence in the global media landscape. His current empire, a misinformation machine that has hoodwinked and misled millions by insidiously disguising propaganda as news, is the unethical culmination of this single-minded pursuit of power at all costs.

Wallabies' media conglomerate has become despised worldwide for its corrosive impact on societies across the globe. His companies have been accused of inflaming cultural divisions, undermining democratic institutions, and even inadvertently causing loss of life by recklessly spreading misinformation and conspiracies. To the nations his media empire has duped, Wallabie is reviled as a modern-day serial deceiver.

Despite this outward persona of the ruthless corporate titan, Wallabies' core motivation has always been rooted in a deep, albeit misguided, desire to secure his family's legacy and respect. His love for Lova, in particular, remains one of the few tethers reminding him of the virtues and values he long abandoned in his quest to amass wealth and power.

The Descent: Increasingly in his twilight years, Wallabie has developed an obsessive fixation on maintaining relevance and leaving an indelible mark on the world before his mortality fades. This pathological desperation has made him increasingly vulnerable to the manipulative machinations of his unscrupulous sons, Edgar and Oliver.

Driven by their own craven self-interests, the manipulative stepbrothers have systematically maneuvered Wallabies into one ethically bankrupt business venture after another, i.e., blood testing. Their latest scheme, the Inadequit hospital chain, and its unproven RED Treatment represent the apex of their ability to gaslight and cajole their aging father into prioritizing profit over human life itself.

Despite Lova's impassioned pleas for him to confront the inevitable catastrophe that awaits, Wallabie remains stubbornly blinded by the intoxicating lure of power and legacy. His misguided male heirs have him so effectively unnerved that even his love for his daughter cannot penetrate the fog of self-delusion.

A Last Bastion of Hope:

If there is one truth Wallabie cannot ignore, it is the pure, ethical love of the wife who challenged his worldview so many years ago. Anneli Persson Richman first encountered the media mogul through an experimental dating site aimed at bringing people of different ideologies and backgrounds together. While Wallabie was reluctantly nudged into joining the unorthodox platform by a concerned daughter from a previous marriage, Anneli actively sought the experience - determined to open her progressive mind to new perspectives. Despite their seemingly incompatible dispositions and significant age gap, Wallabie and Anneli formed an unlikely bond. The Swedish-born academic and humanitarian saw beyond the gruff exterior of the self-made tycoon, believing she could reawaken the inner good within his increasingly materialistic soul. For a time, it seemed Anneli's nurturing wisdom and moral guidance had steered Wallabies away from his worst impulses.

The Reckoning: Now, as things spiral rapidly out of control, Wallabie finds himself at an existential crossroads. The dangers posed by the RED Treatment, combined with the looming consequences of his media empire's propagation of misinformation and hatred, threaten to undermine any remaining semblance of a positive legacy.

It is here, teetering on the precipice of irredeemable infamy, that Wallabie must confront the harsh truth—that the path he chose has not led to the profound patriarchal imprint he sought but rather a slow corrosion of his very soul. The man once driven by a lust for power and wealth now stands face-to-face with his own unforgivable weakness—his inability to withstand the avarice of his own bloodline.

Only by heeding the clarion call for accountability from Lova and Anneli can Wallabie hope to salvage some last vestiges of redemption from the smoldering wreckage of his life's work. The road will not be easy, requiring an acknowledgment of his own culpability in creating an ethical, societal, and journalistic wasteland.

But if there are two truths Wallabie cannot ignore, they are the moral courage of the daughter, who shines like a beacon, and the wife, whose nurturing wisdom beckons him home from the abyss he's created. Whether the media mogul can ultimately overcome his worst impulses to earn their respect may be his final, most crucial test of character.

Anneli Persson Richman

The Principled Anchor

Despite her impressive cache of degrees from prestigious universities, Anneli Persson Richman's true calling has been as a mentor and moral anchor for her powerful family. The Swedish-

Australian woman opted to forgo career ambitions, instead choosing to nurture her globetrotting son Fred and teenage daughter Lova with profound empathy and existential wisdom.

Anneli's expertise lies in the philosophy of existential-phenomenological psychology and the core concept of "thrownness"—the notion that we are all thrust into circumstances beyond our control. Through her teachings, she has helped guide Lova and Fred in finding meaning and ethical purpose despite inheriting the immense privilege and moral hazards surrounding wealth and power.

It was this spiritual generosity that first drew Anneli to her husband, Wallabie Richman, over 17 years ago via an experimental dating platform. Determined to awaken the ethical soul trapped within the gruff media mogul's materialistic pursuits, she embarked on a journey to transform him through nurturing wisdom. For a period, Anneli's presence did steer Wallabie away from his worst impulses and greed-fueled recklessness. But as his business ventures metastasized into a global propaganda empire fraught with unethical practices, her moral unease has grown, particularly over whispers of the disturbing "Project 2025" Wallabie refuses to abandon.

The Tightrope Walker:

Anneli now walks a delicate tightrope, striving to nurture her loved ones while staying unwaveringly true to her own principles. As Wallabie risks everything to chase more wealth through the unproven Inadequit hospital venture, she is achingly aware of the consequences her choices could have on Lova and Fred.

Yet the wise mother also recognizes her husband's need to find his own path, even if it leads him to storms she cannot control. Staying the course as her family's ethical anchor is Anneli's highest priority.

Under her serene exterior lies a wellspring of resilience and an unbending moral compass. She has defied societal expectations to forge a life guided by an unwavering sense of purpose. In the gilded labyrinth of power and wealth, Anneli's wisdom beckons her loved ones to always confront: "Who am I? What is my purpose?"

The Enigmatic Presence: Anneli's profound influence also extends outside her own family through enigmatic ties. She has fostered a deep mentorship with Lova's confidant, Milo Venari, a brilliant mind with potential links to the mysterious Swedish intelligence agency KSI. The extent of Anneli's connection to Milo's covert world remains mysterious.

While her bond with the ever-wandering Fred allows only fleeting maternal moments, Anneli recognizes he is forging his own extraordinary path, guided by her teachings.

In the Richman dynasty's swirling moral grays, Anneli remains a strident beacon of black-and-white ethics. Her life is a testament to the resilience of the human spirit when guided by an unwavering moral compass. By embodying the profound concept of "thrownness," Anneli hopes to steer her family back towards the principles she holds so dear, no matter the personal costs.

Dick-Carl 'Skater' Rovzbush

Codename: The Unrepentant 3

A Toxic Triad Personified

Rovzbush is a domineering presence—the very embodiment of the ruthless operative who deploys any underhanded tactic necessary to attain victory at all costs. He is an unholy amalgamation of three of the modern Republican Party's most notorious figures: the strategic brilliance of Carl, the born-into-privilege recklessness of 43, and the cold, calculated amorality of former Veep, Dick.

This volatile admixture has produced a veritable red giant in the conservative powerbroker realm. Rovzbush personifies the win-at-all-costs mercenary, for whom no ethical line is to be left uncrossed in pursuit of his objectives. His formidable fusion of masterminds makes him an imposing foe for any adversary.

The Fixer's Darkly Comedic Swan Song

Initially taking center stage through his machiavellian machinations, Rovzbush's unexpected demise shifts the narrative focus onto his funeral. But this is no mere mourning; in a darkly satirical twist, the occasion becomes a pivotal investor recruitment drive for the ethically bankrupt Inadequit hospital chain and its nefarious Red Treatment.

Rovzbush's indelible legacy, however, ensures a seamless transition of moral abandonment. His firm Mud, Smear & Fear LLP continues operations as a reality distortion factory, churning out a new generation of protégé operatives to carry on his brand of truth-obfuscating skullduggery on behalf of the highest bidder.

In this purgatory of ethics, no line remains uncrossed, and no tactic is deemed too unscrupulous to deploy. Rovzbush's spiritual progeny honors his memory by perpetuating his ethos, ensuring the noxious cloud of deception he embodied continues to suffocate democracy long after his corporeal departure.

Dick-Carl is a Co-Founder of Mud, Smear & Fear., LLP

When you need a reality distortion partner, call us!

The Next Mark™ Bros. Despicable VC Firm

Summary:

The very name says it all: these venture capitalists, led by the Philter brothers, are singularly focused on identifying their next mark to exploit. Personifying unchecked greed, Jon Jr. and Derrick shamelessly prey on vulnerability to secure investments for their unconscionable pursuits. Banned from their family's businesses due to fraud, the opportunistic siblings have turned their sights to the Inadequit hospital chain. Their goal? Recruiting ultra-wealthy conservative investors to back a for-profit medical sector freed from ethical constraints.

Displaying a startling lack of empathy, the Philter brothers take advantage of the somber backdrop of a funeral to make their pitch. As mourners grieve, these amoral VCs attempt to manipulate their fragile emotional state into funding the

Inadequit scheme and its ethically dubious "personal freedom" treatments.

With confidence and bravado overcompensating for an absence of charisma, the brothers leverage persuasive tactics honed from years of deception. Any ethical concerns about Inadequit's practices are callously disregarded - the lure of profits is all that matters.

Throughout the narrative, The Next Mark™ Bros Despicable VC Firm personifies the collision of capitalistic zeal and personal freedoms taken to dangerous extremes. The Philters' single-minded amorality and ability to exploit others' vulnerability make them formidable antagonists.

Jerkvanka Branding, Marketing, Public Relations, Private Equity, and Genomic Engineering: The Ultimate Power Couple

Founded by Curvanka Philter, daughter of the illustrious Noah Philter, and her husband Jerrick, the Jerkvanka group is a force to be reckoned with. This dynamic duo has taken the world of politics by storm, leaving a trail of bewildered onlookers in their wake.

Rebranding the Republican Party (and the World)

Jerkvanka's crowning achievement, in addition to the red treatment? Transforming the stodgy old Republican Party into the flashy, fascinator-adorned 1864 Monocle Party. This rebranding extravaganza was the brainchild of Curvanka's marketing genius and Jerrick's political prowess, honed during their stint in the Philter administration.

The Monocle: A Symbol of Regression

At the heart of Jerkvanka's rebranding lies the iconic monocle emblem, painstakingly designed by Curvanka herself. This symbol of sophistication (manufactured in China, ironically) represents the party's commitment to bygone eras, traditional values, and the free market. Because what's more nostalgic than a party that champions the interests of the 1%?

A Brand Identity Like No Other

Jerkvanka's team crafted a visual identity that's equal parts steampunk and MAGA. Think logo, color palette, typography, and messaging frameworks that scream, "I'm a proud conservative, but also kind of hipster!" The goal? Repackage conservatism as a modern yet nostalgic return to America's "good ol' days."

Consolidating Power, One Party at a Time

But Jerkvanka's ambitions extend far beyond mere rebranding. They're centralizing all Monocle Party operations under Noah Philter's corporate umbrella, essentially absorbing the GOP into Philter Enterprises. The former president's ultimate goal? Total control over the conservative movement, from branding to fundraising to data operations.

A Legacy of Unorthodoxy

Curvanka and Jerrick may have flopped during their White House stint, but they've left an indelible mark on American politics. They've transformed a major party to reflect one man's regressive, narcissistic vision, potentially hijacking it for his personal fiefdom. In today's hyper-polarized climate, Jerkvanka has elevated political branding to an audacious new frontier of blurring party and corporate lines.

Experts in Everything (and Then Some)

Genomic engineering (yes, Jerkvanka has also developed the revolutionary Red Treatment for Inadequit Healthcare, dad's Obamacare replacement), world peace—you name it, Jerkvanka's got it covered. They're the ultimate power couple, forging a path of absurdity and satire through the world of politics and bootstrapped businesses.

Edgar and Oliver Richman

The ambitious and morally ambiguous stepbrothers of media mogul Wallabie Richman. United by an insatiable thirst for power, they view their aging father as an obstacle to their grand vision for his Global Media empire.

Exploiting Wallabie's fascination with new trends, they convince him to invest in the cutting-edge but risky Inadequit hospital chain and its experimental gene editing treatments. Secretly, they hope the treatment fails, paving their way to seize control. Their machinations are opposed by stepsister Lova, who warns of the dangers and her stepbrothers' ulterior motives. But Wallabie dismisses Lova's concerns, blinded by ego and fear of irrelevance.

As the brothers carefully maneuver into positions of power at TOXic Global Media, aligning with like-minded board members, their ambition has eroded any sense of familial duty.

Lova's opposition is seen as a minor obstacle to be brushed aside in their high-stakes ascent.

With neither ethics nor family loyalty to constrain them, Edgar and Oliver are willing to play a dangerous game of profiting from their father's potential downfall in their ruthless pursuit of dominance over the media empire.

Fred Richman: The Adventurous Narrator

Fred, Lova's twin brother, is the adventurous and enigmatic narrator of EMBRACE THE LIES. Born into the wealthy Richman family, Fred has inherited his mother Anneli's curiosity and his father Wallabie's charm. His globetrotting lifestyle serves as both an escape and a cover for his intriguing connections.

While not as deeply involved as Lova in family affairs, Fred shares some of her concerns about their father's reckless ventures, particularly the Inadequit Healthcare fiasco. His perspective is shaped by cryptic conversations with a mysterious KSI contact, offering tantalizing glimpses into a world of covert operations and political intrigue. Fred's relationship with Milo, Lova's mentor and KSI agent, adds another layer to his understanding. Though less entangled than his sister, Fred's unique position as both insider and outsider makes him the perfect narrator for this tale of family drama and political satire.

Lester Canda

A protégé of the nefarious operative Dick-Carl "Skater" Rovzbush. Canda was marinated in the underhanded ways of the political underworld from a young age. A regular attendee at the elite's secret conclaves, some whisper he's one of the six masterminds behind the democracy-undermining Project 2025 agenda.

Despite being a notorious golf hack and reckless driver—with four DWIs swept under the rug by parsing words about it being "when he was younger" (as in, yesterday) and invoking his idols George W. Bush and Dick Cheney's DWI arrest histories as precedent—on that he was hired - Canda remains an invaluable asset to the reality distortion firm Mud, Smear & Fear LLP.

His villa on Laughing Waters Beach serves as a retreat but is also perhaps a waystation monitored by the enigmatic Swedish intelligence agency KSI. Whether Canda is an unwitting asset or a Rovzbush mole inside the guild remains uncertain.

What's clear is his status as a red giant in the firmament of conservative deception architects. His unrepentant amorality and mastery of disinformation make him a powerful conduit for sowing chaos and eroding democratic norms on behalf of his shadowy benefactors.

LSIG Agents

LSIG's Undercover Evolutionaries

They could be beachgoers, TV personalities, or even golf pros. But these everyday folks are actually undercover agents for the secret group LSIG, working with the mysterious KSI agency. Their mission? Help make the world more accepting for everyone. Like chameleons, they blend in seamlessly, even at fancy resorts for the rich and powerful. By getting 'dates' and jobs at these places, they can snoop unnoticed. When the elite has private talks, the agents carefully record what's said. They smuggle this intel to LSIG using clever tricks - coded golf bags, homing finches carrying tiny data chips, even truth serum sprays disguised as drink service.

These agents come from all over and speak many languages. But they share one core belief: that we're all equal, just temporary sparks of life. So, they're devoted to protecting diversity and making sure everyone is treated fairly. Working secretly in plain sight, LSIG's revolutionaries are like guardians. What is their extraordinary purpose? Stopping the spread of hatred and lies that threaten our shared humanity. Connected to the enigmatic KSI, this unassuming network has a powerful mission: keeping the positive evolution of society on track, one undercover operation at a time.

The Pepsid Brothers

Rich, Richer, Richest, and Richy—second-generation billionaire brothers and staunch conservatives. They believe in laissez-faire capitalism and limited government, driving their every action.

Motivations & Goals

The Pepsid brothers are motivated by a deep-seated conviction that government regulation infringes on personal liberty and economic freedom. Their ultimate goal is to minimize the government's role, fostering a utopia where individuals and corporations thrive unrestrained.

Background

Exposed to their strict businessman father's conservative teachings, they developed an early aversion to government intervention. They amassed vast wealth through investments and business ventures, establishing a formidable political machine bankrolled by their billions.

Influence & Projects

The Pepsid brothers played a pivotal role in funding the Tee Party movement (aptly named after planned golf resorts), opposing increased government spending and regulation. Their grand plan, Project 2025, aims to shrink the federal government by 50% and abolish all regulatory agencies in 2025.

Personal Lives

The Pepsid Brothers, paragons of modesty, generously offer to send their offspring to exclusive global summer camps—a mere trifle for their humble fortunes. These pillars of restraint are renowned for their "Reaganesque 2 Yachting" lifestyle, each brother boasting two opulent vessels. In a nod to practicality, their main yachts stand exactly 100 times taller than their owners—because who doesn't need a boat that doubles as a skyscraper?

These floating palaces are dutifully trailed by 250-foot support yachts, an absolute necessity for the everyday billionaire. In an eco-friendly gesture, all eight vessels cruise ceaselessly, crowning the Pepsids as world leaders in fossil fuel consumption. How convenient that they're their own best customers! Whispers in high society suggest that come 2026, a third "zoo yacht" will join each fleet, reportedly featuring ostriches in a bizarre nod to the latest GOP mascot rumors.

Relationships

They maintain close relationships with like-minded politicians and corporate lobbyists, advancing their agenda through a web of influence. However, their political beliefs often divide them from their more progressive children and grandchildren.

Notable Achievements

The Pepsid brothers excel at Constitutional Scrabble, redefining the nation's founding documents to align with their agenda. In a remarkable display of camaraderie, they take turns winning the championships of Constitutional Scrabble, often competing against Supreme Court judges who share their ideology. The brothers are renowned champions at Devolution Plateau Resorts. As their wealth and influence grow, their unwavering conservatism guides increasingly audacious efforts to dismantle government and reshape society along with libertarian ideals. This provokes a growing backlash from supporters of strong oversight and social safety nets.

Jerry Mander

Summary: Jerry Mander, aka Gerry, is a mastermind of electoral manipulation who has made a career out of shaping the electorate to his advantage. His notorious tactics, which involved parsing demographics and geographical borders using questionable legal tactics, have become synonymous with electoral manipulation. In fact, his success in this field was so profound that the term "gerrymandering" was coined in his "honor" by Dick-Carl 'Skater' Rovzbush in a notable election.

Character:

- **Name:** Gerry Mander

- **Age:** 58

- **Occupation:** Board member of The Next Mark Bros. Despicable VC Firm, board member of numerous conservative think tanks, employee of Mud, Smear, & Fear., LLP

- **Personality:** Arrogant, manipulative, power-hungry

Background:

Jerry's downfall began with a peculiar video game he found as a child, "I Want to Become a Villain." The game's twisted logic brainwashed him into believing that the only way to succeed was to become a villain. As he grew older, he became increasingly manipulative and deceitful, eventually entering politics to maximize his influence.

Gerrymandering:

Jerry's primary goal is to manipulate electoral districts to give his political party an unfair advantage and dilute the voting power of minority groups. He achieves this by parsing demographics and geographical borders, using questionable legal tactics to shape the electorate just the way he wants. His tactics are designed to protect incumbents, amplify his party's voice, and silence opposing voices. Despite widespread condemnation, Jerry remains unapologetic, driven by an insatiable ambition for power and control.

Impact:

Gerrymandering has far-reaching consequences, undermining the integrity of elections and eroding public trust in democratic institutions. It distorts the will of the people, reduces the power of minority groups, and polarizes politics. Jerry Mander's legacy is a testament to the dangers of unchecked ambition and the erosion of democratic values.

Jerry is a red giant :)

George P. Noonan

Summary:

George P. Noonan is the culmination of the most influential voices that propelled the 43rd Administration to power despite its leader's glaring inadequacies. This amalgamation of intellectuals, talk show hosts, opinion editors, and writers represents the collective guilt and hubris that led to one of the most disastrous presidencies in American history.

Character:

- **Name:** George P. Noonan

- **Age:** 76

- **Occupation:** Former opinion editor, writer, and TV personality

- **Personality:** Arrogant, self-assured, and remorseful

Background:

George P. Noonan was the embodiment of the elite media class that championed the 43rd Administration's rise to power. With his silver tongue and polished prose, he convinced millions of Americans that the unqualified candidate was the right choice for the job. As the administration's policies imploded, George and his cohorts remained steadfast in their support, peddling propaganda and half-truths to the masses.

Guilt and Redemption:

As the administration's failures mounted, George's conscience began to stir. He now appears on progressive TV shows, espousing a newfound sense of guilt and responsibility for his role in shaping public opinion. His words are laced with regret, but it's unclear whether he's too late or genuine. Has he truly changed, or is he merely attempting to salvage his legacy?

Legacy of 43:

The 43rd Administration's legacy seemed impossible to outdo in terms of sheer incompetence and disaster. However,

Noah Philter, the current nominee, has managed to equal, if not surpass, the 43rd's catastrophic record. George P. Noonan's influence, along with that of his ilk, helped pave the way for this catastrophe. They created a political environment where a candidate like Noah Philter could thrive, and now they're left to grapple with the consequences of their actions.

Impact:

George P. Noonan's actions, and those of his peers, have had a lasting impact on American politics. They helped propel the GOP toward the edge of obsolescence, clearing the path for the likes of Noah Philter to rise to power. The consequences of their hubris will be felt for generations to come.

Inadequit Healthcare Systems

Inadequit Healthcare Systems Group: A Masterstroke.

Twice-impeached former president Noah Philter's long-awaited answer to "repeal and replace" Obamacare has finally arrived: the Inadequit Healthcare Systems Group. This farcical operation is Philter's vision for healthcare reform, brought to you by a cabal of ultra-wealthy opportunists who view medical ethics as an inconvenience.

The Flagship Hospitals: Modernity

Inadequit's flagship hospitals. All 150 are sleek glass-and-steel edifices beckoning the wealthy and credulous with promises of "cutting-edge care." But behind that gleaming facade lurks a cold, 'seemingly' sterile lobby devoid of human staff - manned instead by a battalion of humanoid robots, the unblinking face of Philter's Orwellian healthcare dystopia.

The Red Procedure: A Miracle Cure Bred in Squalor

The crown jewel is the "Red Procedure"—a gene-editing protocol that, according to charlatan Philter and his progeny, allows full recovery from any surgery or ailment within just four hours! But this "miracle cure" germinated not in a prestigious lab but in the neglected, mold-infested bowels of the laughably named "Tangerine Medical University."

From Scam to Sham

Tangerine was originally Philter's failed real estate university—shut down so hastily that half-eaten cafeteria meals still moldered on trays when the quacks moved in. With stunning disregard for sanitization, they converted these squalid remnants into a biomedical Frankenlab devoted to developing the Red Treatment in secret.

Unsanitary? Just Call It Cost-Cutting!

The charlatans chose unbridled cost-cutting over hygiene, developing the Red Procedure using an all-robot workforce assembled on-site to eliminate "skilled medical labor." Bonus freebie: the Sporebourne Virusx, born from the neglected detritus of the former campus and hitching a ride onto the robots, for national distribution to all INADEQUIT HEALTHCARE Hospitals.

The Investors: Profiting from Pandemonium

Inadequit's esteemed investors include Wallabie, a hospital exec named "Scotty Rickless Dick," the Despicable VC grifters, the notorious Vaccum & Ruen Equity vultures, and, of course, former Grifter-in-Chief Noah Philter himself. But don't worry; these upstanding entrepreneurs know better than to partake in their own medical malpractice; they hightail it to Switzerland or Sweden when they need quality care.

The Experts: Unqualified By Design

Who are the true "experts" behind this shambolic operation? None other than Philter's daughter Curvanka and her husband—two wildly unqualified people who somehow became the medical masterminds spearheading the Red Procedure's development. Credentials? Newly minted Genomic Engineers, but who needs 'em when you've got a famous last name like "Philter"?

The Hype Campaign

While the charlatans at Tangerine developed their virus-laced procedure in secrecy, the hype campaign was unfolding on the public stage. A giddy Noah Philter (granted a nice slice of equity) and his cronies at TOXic Friends Global Media drummed up investors and conservative pundits eager to partake in this "life-changing" healthcare freedom opportunity. 150 Inadequit hospitals opened nationwide on the same day, ready to unleash untold consequences on thousands of the nation's wealthiest citizens seeking Philter's warped version of treatment.

So book your freedom Red Procedure at Inadequit Healthcare today! After all, replacing that pesky Obamacare with reckless medical mayhem, neglectful practices, and potential viral pandemics is exactly what America's been clamoring for, right? What could possibly go wrong?

Warning: This entire operation is satirical fiction and in no way based on actual science or real medical practices. Do not attempt any part of the Red Procedure at home or seek treatment at Inadequit Healthcare. You've been warned.

Tangerine R&D University — See INADEQUIT HEALTHCARE SYSTEMS.

Devolution Plateau Resorts & Spas

The places where conservative conclaves, summits, conferences, and powwows take place and anti-progress is planned to wind our country backward.

The Never-Ending Milkshake

All vessels can make one slurp at some point.

Courtrooms

Noah's the court jester's playground.

Stormy Sirens℠

Velvet Storm's elite escort agency, Stormy Sirens ℠ provided elite companions to the wealthy and powerful. After a 2016 rendezvous with Noah Philter, Velvet's services became coveted at ultra-conservative events hosted by the 1864 Monocle Party. Stunning "Sirens" embodied Republican patriarchs' fantasies at these debauched galas.

As their presence became an open secret, the Sirens satirized the moral hypocrisy they served. However, when exposed in 2024, Velvet was portrayed negatively, prompting her outraged Senate run to reshape her legacy and fight for sex workers' rights. Noah takes credit for her business success and demands a 7% royalty on her services.

The Leading 'Conservative' politicians.

The Philter Sycophants: A Menagerie of Spineless Wonders

Welcome to the circus of Noah Philter's most devoted bootlickers! Leading this parade of moral bankruptcy is Glitch McDonnell, the 'super' senior senator from Kentucky. Not content with merely obstructing progress, Glitch hijacked the Supreme Court nomination process, gifting Philter a legacy of partisan justices that will echo through generations.

At the center of this ethical wasteland stands Gwet Nitwich, the crown jewel of political depravity. A true Red Giant, Nitwich has single-handedly accelerated the GOP's descent into madness. This master of self-serving duplicity has elevated disingenuousness to an art form, flip-flopping faster than a fish out of water while lining his own pockets.

Orbiting these twin black holes of integrity are the usual suspects: Lady G, VD Lance, Barr Billy, Kevin McCutie, Gov. Boots, the forgettable New Hampshire Gov., Shcott "Moon" Walker, Ted Marco Ruse, O'Josh Haulinas, and Indy Penceadent. Each, in their own pathetic way, contributes to the spectacular implosion of democratic norms.

Watch as they perform amazing feats of mental gymnastics, contorting themselves to fit whatever shape Philter, McDonnell, and Nitwich demand. It's a spectacle of sycophancy that would be hilarious if it weren't so terrifying!

And now, enjoy the sight of these political acrobats perched precariously on the sharp white picket fences Noah Philter has so generously provided. From this uncomfortable vantage point, they clap like trained seals, cheering on their master as he brazenly cheats his way through another round of golf. It's a fitting metaphor for their careers—painful, pointless, and ultimately self-destructive.

GOP Grand Old Pachyderms

The Battle for an Iconic Emblem

Once a symbol of unity and wisdom, the GOP's elephant emblem has been tarnished by divisive tactics and ideological betrayal. Activist groups Save Our Elephants and Respect Our Elephants are fighting to sever the elephant's ties to the GOP's sullied reputation, sparking a nationwide call for authenticity in political representation.

The legal battle has reached the Supreme Court, where the justices are grappling with the ethics of historical symbols used out of step with their essence. The fate of the elephant emblem hangs in the balance as the court deliberates on the future of this iconic symbol.

Will the GOP be forced to redefine itself, or will the elephant remain a symbol of the party's legacy? The outcome of this landmark case remains uncertain, but one thing is clear: the future of political representation hangs in the balance. George W. Bush mortally wounded the GOP. Philter made it extra dead, the GOP.

1724 Kingservative Party

The 1724 Kingservative Party: A Guide to the Retrograde Revolution

Welcome to the Kingservative Party, where the motto is "No rights for you!" This radical faction emerged as a response to the "too woke" 1864 Monocle Party, seeking to drag the country back to the dark ages of the 18th century.

Their vision? In a world where only rich white men hold power and democracy, human rights and women's rights are mere fantasies. Public schools? Closed. Government agencies like the EPA, Education Department, and FDA? Abolished. Women's right to vote? Revoked.

The Kingservatives proudly wear coonskin caps, symbolizing their rejection of progress and embrace of a caveman mentality. Their mascot, the raccoon, represents their commitment to ignorance and regression.

But the Kingservatives are not alone in their quest for retrograde dominance. They're embroiled in a never-ending "battle royal" lawsuit with their ideological foes, the 1864 Monocle Party and the old GOP (the Grand Ole Pachyderms). The three groups are locked in a vicious struggle for control of the conservative narrative, each trying to outdo the others in their rejection of progress and equality.

Will the Kingservatives emerge victorious, imposing their draconian vision on the country? Or will the Monocle Party's nostalgia for the 19th century prevail? Perhaps the Grand Ole Pachyderms will find a way to reclaim their lost glory and restore the GOP to its former grandeur.

One thing is certain: The outcome of this lawsuit will determine the course of American history. Will the country move forward, or will it be dragged backward into the dark ages?

Project 2025

Project 2025: A Descent into Anarchy and Unfreedom

The modern conservative parties have unleashed a radical initiative, Project 2025, which threatens to dismantle the country's regulatory framework, eliminate government agencies, and strip citizens of their protections. This extreme plan leads us down the treacherous road to unfreedom.

Key Objectives:

- Dismantle government agencies, including the EPA, Department of Education, and FDA.

- Repeal crucial regulations, such as the Clean Air Act and the Civil Rights Act.

- Eliminate social safety nets, including Social Security, Medicare, and Medicaid.

- Allow corporations to exploit the environment and workers without consequence.

- Implement a surveillance state to monitor and control citizens.

The Fascism Virus:

This initiative is one of the many viruses that Noah Philter and his ilk have unleashed on our country, infecting the minds of some with a toxic ideology that prioritizes corporate interests over human well-being. The fascism virus has spread rapidly, exploiting the vulnerabilities of our democratic system.

Consequences:

- Environmental catastrophe and ecological devastation

- Widening wealth gaps and economic inequality

- Suppression of scientific progress and critical thinking

- Authoritarian rule and the death of democracy

- Chaos and anarchy in the streets

Resistance is Crucial: The fate of American democracy hangs in the balance. It is imperative that citizens, activists, and progressive forces unite to thwart Project 2025 and preserve the principles of freedom, equality, and justice.

Guilds of Good

Guilds of Good: A Call to Action for the Cognizant Youth

The cognizant youth face a multitude of concerns that threaten our society. Climate change, systemic injustices, and environmental degradation ravage our planet. Meanwhile, a select few enjoy luxurious lifestyles, like two yachts in use at the same time, one to follow the other, equipped with an endless supply of toilet paper. They've got the means to live lavishly, while many are marginalized, ostracized, and treated unfairly. We're all connected, comprised of the same fundamental building blocks—molecules that make up every living thing. This realization should instill a sense of unity and shared humanity, where every individual deserves a place in this world. It should be self-evident that all men and women are created equal, yet we still struggle to uphold this fundamental principle. I remember the kindergarten days when children of all races, demographics, and ethnic backgrounds played together in harmony. They laughed, giggled, and got along beautifully without a care in the world. What happens as we grow older? Why do we let our differences tear us apart?

Some of us, the cognizant among us, haven't forgotten those carefree days. We remember the joy of unity, the beauty of diversity, and the simplicity of getting along. Just as Darwin's finches adapted their beaks to the food available on the Galapagos Islands, we must evolve faster to respond to the challenges of our time. But instead, we're devolving. Recently, women's rights have been rolled back more than 50 years, taking away reproductive healthcare and fundamental human rights. This is unacceptable.

The Guilds of Good will not stand for it. We will not stand idly by as our society takes steps backward. We will not tolerate the hoarding of resources, the oppression of marginalized communities, and the denial of basic human rights. We must evolve, not devolve. We must work together to create a better world where every individual has access to the resources they need to thrive. But how can we evolve when the resources we need are hoarded by those who prioritize grotesque wealth accumulation? The elders, bent on building their fortunes, seem oblivious to the struggles of the present. Trillions of dollars are stored in offshore banks, in the "cloud," and in other hidden vaults reserved for future generations while we're left to fight over crumbs. Meanwhile, some people just go on slurping from their "endless" milkshakes, oblivious to the world burning around them. They claim that's just the way it's always been, that resources will never run out, and that they'll always have enough to live lavishly. But we know the truth—that many trillions are socked away, unused, and unshared while the majority struggle to make ends meet.

The Guilds of Good are just the beginning of a movement, but we're faced with a harsh reality: we lack resources and have no idea how to access the funds needed to make the wholesale changes our world so desperately needs. We're not naive; we know that some people do well with their wealth, but we also know that many trillions are locked away, inaccessible to those who need them most. We must find a way to unlock these resources, to fuel our dreams, and to create a better world for all.

Vacuum & Ruen Equity

Vaccum & Ruen: The Private Equity Company You Love to Hate

Private equity investing has taken over our country, and it's not all good. These companies make money by buying up businesses, cutting costs, and selling them for a profit. But what's the cost? Jobs are lost, communities are hurt, and essential services are compromised. That's where Vaccum & Ruen come in—the private equity company that's making a killing in the healthcare industry. Their latest target? A couple of chains of hospitals that they extracted profits from and then let fall into ruin. But don't worry, they didn't leave them to die. Another division of their company swooped in, picked them up out of insolvency, and is now bringing them back to life under the "Inadequit Healthcare" model. That's right, they're profiting from both ends.

And it gets even better. They're partnering with the Despicable Brothers, Noah Philter, and Wallabie as celebrity investors, and they are granting them extra equity for their fame and ability to amplify the message through TOXic's megaphone. Hedge Hog, another equity company, is also on board. Together, they're pushing the narrative that AI is the answer to every problem, no matter the human cost.

Their plan? Bring in AI and robotics to run the entire hospital group—150 units strong. Robotic nurses, doctors, and oversight robots will be taking over, with robots overseeing robots from overseas and elsewhere. They're convinced that AI will fix everything without considering the devastating impact on real people's lives. What could possibly go wrong? They invest with Hedge Hog IP.

Conclave Summits

The Conclave Playbook: Unveiling the Secrets of Minority Rule

What is a Conclave?

A conclave is a clandestine gathering of the GOP's elite, where the masters of manipulation converge to orchestrate the future of American politics and law. Behind closed doors, they scheme to maintain their grip on power, exploiting loopholes and manipulating the system to ensure minority rule.

Notable Conclaves

- **The Devolution Resort and Spas:** Where the 1% Plot to Subvert Democracy: A luxurious getaway at the posh Devolution Resort and Spa, where the GOP's power brokers gather to undermine progressive values and consolidate their control.

- **Where Corpus Linguistics Meets Conservative Ideology:** A conclave held at the swanky Disinformation Spa and Retreat, featuring Judge Peeless and other conservative legal scholars who will instruct on how to wield corpus linguistics as a tool to justify their ideological agenda.

The True Purpose of Conclaves

Conclaves are not just exclusive gatherings of like-minded individuals; they are strategic planning sessions to:

- **Gerrymander Districts:** Manipulate electoral boundaries to ensure GOP dominance.

- **Stack the Courts:** Appoint conservative judges who will interpret the law in favor of the GOP's interests.

- **Disenfranchise Voters:** Implement voter suppression tactics to limit the influence of progressive voters.

- **Shape Public Opinion:** Craft narratives and propaganda to sway public opinion in favor of the GOP's agenda.

The Conclave's Impact on American Democracy

By manipulating the system and exploiting loopholes, the GOP's conclave attendees have successfully:

- **Eroded Voting Rights:** Disenfranchised millions of Americans, particularly minorities and low-income citizens.

- **Entrenched Minority Rule:** Ensured that a minority of the population holds disproportionate power and influence.

- **Undermined the Judiciary:** Appointed judges who prioritize ideology over justice, leading to a biased and unfair legal system.

The Conclave's Legacy

The GOP's conclave attendees have left an indelible mark on American politics, perpetuating a system of minority rule and undermining the principles of democracy. As the veil of secrecy surrounding these gatherings is lifted, it becomes clear that the true purpose of conclaves is to maintain power at any cost, even if it means subverting the will of the people.

Ursula, see LSIG

Red treatment

Gene editing via The Red Treatment: The Top Secret Answer to Obamacare

Over the past two decades, wealthy conservative media personalities have pushed a narrative of personal freedom without collective responsibility. Ironically, these very talking heads now have an exclusive opportunity to be the first patients at Inadequit Healthcare System's new hospitals—facilities that embody the ethos of unbridled personal choice.

The main attraction? The Red Treatment is a supposedly revolutionary and proprietary gene editing procedure. Many pundits, eager to validate their on-air rants, have signed up to undergo this "freedom treatment" on a live stream for all to see.

Experience true healthcare freedom with the Red Treatment! This cutting-edge gene editing procedure ensures you recover from any procedure, invasive or not, in a mere 4 hours. No more lengthy hospital stays or grueling rehabilitation. You'll be back on your feet, ready to conquer the world, in no time.

But there's more—the Red Treatment allows you to be a pioneer by opting out of anesthesia. Embrace the thrill of feeling every incision and stitch. It's an unparalleled experience that will leave you feeling truly alive. Administered by highly advanced robots overseen by not one but two additional layers of robot overseers, the Red Treatment guarantees precision, efficiency, and unprecedented care. Our robotic staff will monitor your entire journey. Imagine freedom from tedious protocols, nagging doctors, and caring nurses. The Red Treatment reality: no hand-washing, no masks, and no healthcare follow-up visits to worry about.

While investors like Noah Philter cautiously seek traditional care in Switzerland or Sweden, the Red Treatment is a marvel few are ready to embrace. But for the pioneers craving ultimate healthcare liberty, it's the answer you've been waiting for. Say goodbye to the shackles of Obamacare and hello to a new world of complete control over your health. What are you waiting for? Take the leap and experience the thrilling convenience of the Red Treatment today!

Administration Options

- **Red Pill:** Swallow a single red pill to trigger the advanced programming embedded within.

- **Red Ultraviolet Light:** A red ultraviolet light suppository inserted directly into the rectum by gentle robotic assistants.

WARNING: The red treatment presented here is a malicious promotion concocted by the TOXic Friends Global Media team. Their insidious ability to manipulate beliefs extends to inciting individuals to act against their own well-being, a testament to the potency of this high-level virus. This powerful procedure may cause temporary side effects, like heightened temporary euphoria. Use at your own risk.

SCOTUS team

The Supreme Court of the United States (SCOTUS) has been compromised by a shocking arrangement involving Noah Philter, a powerful figure with questionable motives. Several justices owe their positions to "Glitch McDonnell stolen picks," originally intended for President Obama's nominees. These justices have become beholden to Philter, serving as indentured servants at his Doral golf course as part of their membership. To ensure their availability, they reside at Doral Villas, a convenient distance from Philter's command center. But that's not all—these captive judges commute to Washington, D.C., in style, courtesy of a bevy of benevolent billionaires who lend them their private jets. A fleet of luxurious aircraft awaits them at a nearby jetport, where they can indulge in a "menu of jets" every morning. No strings attached, of course. From Gulfstreams to Falcons, they simply pick their poison and soar into the nation's capital, ready to render judgments that align with Philter's interests.

This clandestine arrangement has far-reaching implications, contributing to the phenomenon of minority rule in the United States.

By manipulating the highest court in the land, Philter and his allies have hijacked the democratic process, undermining the principles of fair representation and accountability. As a result, the country is governed in a manner that favors the interests of a select few rather than the will of the people. This disturbing reality has severe consequences for the nation's governance, threatening the very foundations of American democracy.

Fascism – a virus

Definition

Fascism is a type of government or political system that is very controlling and often violent. It is usually led by a strong leader who has total power and control over the country. Fascist governments often use fear, propaganda, and violence to keep people in line and get what they want. Dictators.

Characteristics

- **Authoritarian:** Fascist governments are led by a strong leader who has total power and control.

- **Nationalist:** Fascist governments often focus on the idea that their country is superior to others and that they need to protect it from outsiders.

- **Anti-Democratic**: Fascist governments do not believe in giving people the right to vote or participate in government.

- **Violent:** Fascist governments often use violence and intimidation to get what they want.

- **Racist**: Fascist governments often believe in the idea of racial superiority, which means they think one race is better than others.

The Creeping Threat of Fascism

In our story, Noah Philter's rhetoric and policies have seemed to let the virus of fascism creep into society. His divisive language and authoritarian tendencies have created an environment where hate and intolerance can thrive. This is not just a fictional concern but a real threat to our democracy and our values.

The Warning Signs

As we navigate the world of "Political Lust," it's essential to recognize the warning signs of fascism. We must be vigilant against the erosion of civil liberties, the suppression of dissenting voices, and the demonization of marginalized groups. We must also be aware of the ways in which fear, propaganda, and misinformation can be used to manipulate public opinion and undermine our democracy.

The Antidote: Voting

But there is hope. The antidote to the virus of fascism is voting. By exercising our right to vote, we can hold our leaders accountable and ensure that our government remains a democracy of the people, by the people, and for the people. Voting is a powerful tool that allows us to shape our future and reject the divisive and harmful ideologies of fascism.

The Power of the Ballot

When we vote, we are not just casting a ballot; we are exercising our power as citizens. We are saying that we will not be swayed by fear and propaganda and that we will stand up for our values and our rights. We are saying that we believe in the principles of democracy and that we will fight to protect them.

Let's Use Our Power

So, let's use our power. Let's vote in every election, from local to national. Let's educate ourselves on the issues and the candidates. Let's hold our leaders accountable and demand that they represent our evolved values and our interests. By doing so, we can create a society that is just, equitable, and free from the threat of fascism.

Easter eggs, did you find any?

Steele Michele

Steele Michele fancies himself a reformed conservative, lamenting the Republican Party's descent into the farcical 1864 Monocle Party. Yet the former RNC chair conveniently omits his own role in paving the way for the monstrous Noah Philter nomination in 2016. Now, he traipses the talk show circuit, decrying the very forces he once eagerly harnessed.

However, the political operatives still welcome Michele into their inner sanctums—not for his rhetoric but for his prowess on the golf course. His formidable game guarantees victory in the recreational pursuits that matter most to the graying eminences.

Unbeknownst to them, Michele's own son Jordan runs the world's most popular progressive blog, leaking details from those very conclaves his father attends. While the patriarch preaches about reasonable conservatism, it's the hacker son's keyboards that are paving an actual progressive paradise—the ultimate form of redemption.

Constitutional Scrabble

Constitutional Scrabble: A Game of Linguistic Dominance

In this satirical world, Constitutional Scrabble is a twisted game where the nation's founding documents are manipulated to suit personal agendas. Richest Pepsid and Tick Granite, the supreme champions, wield their linguistic prowess like a weapon against democracy. They reshape the Constitution's words to align with their ultra-conservative agenda, threatening the foundations of democracy.

The game is a battleground where the nation's fate hangs in the balance. Each move carries profound consequences as the players seek to reshape the nation's destiny, one letter at a time. The Pepsid brothers and their allies excel at this game, manipulating words and phrases to fit their narrative. Constitutional Scrabble is a hybrid of Scrabble and corpus linguistics, where words are atomized and reconstructed to mean anything desired. The game is played by lawyers and judges who hire experts to help them twist the Constitution's words to fit their agenda. The Philter brothers, Jon Jr. and Derrick languish at the bottom, their ineptitude at the game mirroring their failings in business and golf.

COVID-19 - a virus!

If the United States had responded to COVID-19 like Australia, around 900,000 American (more) lives could have been saved. While Australia implemented strict lockdowns, closed businesses and borders, and followed scientific advice, the Philter administration downplayed the threat. President Noah Philter called it a "hoax" and suggested injecting disinfectants into the nether regions, as his officials fed conspiracy theories to supporters via TOXic Friends News. Australia's unified, expert-guided pandemic strategy was fiendishly simple yet impossible for the intellectually barren Philter, whose policies resembled psychiatric finger-paintings—shut down one day, reopen the next, mixed messages on masks. Though Australia's island geography helped, the US could've tried harder than having their unhinged president babble about "nuking the hurricane" of a virus. Nine hundred thousand preventable deaths are no laughing matter, but such dark humor captures the tragic mismanagement that devastated American families.

Vaccines

Really, are they needed? Vote, use your hard-fought rights, and be the master antidote.

Mud, Smear & Fear., LLP

Co-Founders: Dick-Carl "Skater' Rovzbush, Tick Granite

Political operatives seeking dirty tricks and mudslinging come to us. Our services include:

- Dirty tricks and sabotage

- Mudslinging and negative campaigns

- Fear-mongering and voter manipulation

- Political strategy and media manipulation

- Opposition research and backchanneling

With 25+ years of experience, a proven success rate, and discretion guaranteed, we're the go-to partner for reality distortion. Call us to tarnish reputations and sway votes.

Conservative Battle

Conservative Chaos: EMBRACE THE VIRUS

The GOP's possible loss of the elephant symbol sparks an epic battle for the party's new identity. Two factions emerge: the 1864 Monocle Party, led by former President Noah Philter, and the 1724 Kingservative Party. The Monocles want to return to the gilded age, while the Kingservatives seek to drag the party back to an era before women's suffrage. The legal battle is marked by absurdity, with both sides employing underhanded tactics. An online game pits the Monocle ostrich against the Kingservative raccoon, with billionaires and trillionaires funding the fight. As the nation looks on in amusement, satirists and comedians revel in the ridiculousness. Will the Monocle ostrich or Kingservative raccoon win? One thing is certain: the battle for conservatism has descended into a circus of epic proportions.

1864 Monocle Party

Imagine a political party that's so out of touch that they make the dinosaurs look progressive. Welcome to the 1864 Monocle Party, where the rich and powerful want to turn back the clock to the "good old days" of aristocracy and social Darwinism.

Their symbol? The ostrich, aptly nicknamed "O'Josh" after Senator Josh Haulinas, who famously ran away from the Capitol riot on January 6th. Just like Haulinas, the Monocles want to bury their heads in the sand and ignore the problems of society. Climate change? What is climate change? Racial injustice? Doesn't exist! Gender equality? Ha! They're too busy prancing around, pretending to be the 'man.'

Their leader, Noah Philter, is a master of absurdity, trading in the GOP's elephant symbol for a tacky ostrich wearing a monocle. It's a party that's all about devolving into the past, where the wealthy elite can rule with an iron fist. Join the Monocles in their bizarre journey back in time, where ignorance is bliss, and the rest of us are just along for the ridiculous ride.

Tick Granite: The Manipulator's Manipulator

Tick Granite, the quintessential political operative, has been a master of dirty tricks and disinformation for decades. Hailing from the Bronx, this "red-giant" of conservative powerbrokers offers his unscrupulous services to the highest bidder. Paradoxically, despite his manipulative prowess, Tick is easily swayed by promises of greater power and influence.

Pardoned 3 times in 4 years (busy guy) by Noah Philter for past misdeeds, Tick now awaits marching orders from Mud, Smear & Fear, LLP. His nickname stems from his persistence and his friends' wives' opinions of his intellect. Working alongside Dick-Carl and Lester, Tick has engineered countless elections through nefarious means.

A whore for money and power, Tick Granite embodies the corrosive influence of unethical politics in a democracy.

Chip and Mookie: The Golf Analysts

Meet Chip and Mookie, the dynamic duo of golf commentary who've traded stuffy country clubs for the wild world of the Kruger-Dunning Orange Slice Golf Classic and forthcoming events. Chip, a former pro golf announcer, was infamously ousted from the majors after his ill-fated "bikini-waxed greens" comment sent sponsors into a tizzy. Mookie, his quick-witted partner, specializes in turning golf jargon into double entendres.

Together, they bring a refreshing dose of irreverence to the staid world of golf. Whether they're analyzing Noah Philter's creative scoring or mocking the 1864 Monocle Party, Chip and

Mookie keep audiences tuned in with their unfiltered commentary.

Look for our main novel in the series, EMBRACE THE VIRUSES.

See how this all ties together in our absurd, dystopian, satirical novel.

Vote for democracy and the rule of law.

Thank you.

Read or listen to EMBRACE THE VIRUSES.

9 7 9 8 3 3 0 5 9 5 8 5 3